W9-BKG-218

LP WES WEL   LR   2/14

Wells, Lee E.,
Incident at Warbow

Donated by
Friends of the Nature Coast
Lakes Region Library

INCIDENT at
WARBOW

Center Point
Large Print

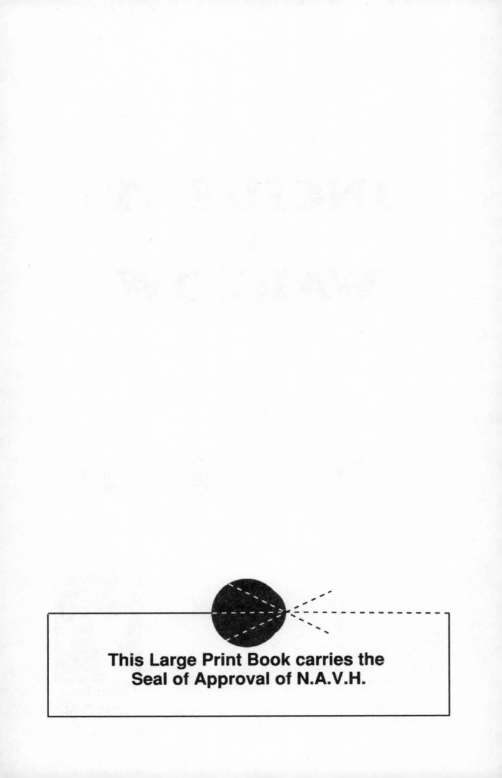

**This Large Print Book carries the
Seal of Approval of N.A.V.H.**

INCIDENT at WARBOW

Lee E. Wells

CENTER POINT LARGE PRINT
THORNDIKE, MAINE

LP WES
LR

This Center Point Large Print edition is published
in the year 2013 by arrangement with
Golden West Literary Agency.

The text of this Large Print edition is unabridged.
In other aspects, this book may vary
from the original edition.
Printed in the United States of America
on permanent paper.
Set in 16-point Times New Roman type.

ISBN: 978-1-61173-895-7

Library of Congress Cataloging-in-Publication Data

Wells, Lee E., 1907–1982.
  Incident at Warbow / Lee. E. Wells. — Center Point Large Print
    edition.
  pages ; cm
  ISBN 978-1-61173-895-7 (library binding : alk. paper)
  1. Large type books. I. Title.
  PS3545.E5425I54 2013
  813′.54—dc23
                                                    2013019091

INCIDENT at WARBOW

Chapter I

The collection of false-front stores and low frame houses crouched under the awesome sweep of the Wyoming land and sky. The town looked as if it had heedlessly dropped out of the bag of some planetary devil who hadn't bothered to come back and scrape it up. Ugly and forlorn, it waited in an endless limbo, saved from complete oblivion by the signs on either end of the orange and black station beside the double line of gleaming rails that came out of nowhere from the east and disappeared into nowhere in the west.

A dirt road came up from the south, crossed the rails and disappeared over the horizon to the north. Moving away from the town, a stagecoach sped northward, leaving a lonesome, spiraling lift of dust that slowly, wearily, settled earthward.

Just within the doorway of the station, a tall man in travel-stained clothes watched until the stagecoach finally became a speck far to the north. The man sighed wearily and looked eastward. He could not even see the hoped-for smudge of smoke against the far horizon.

He shoved hands in the pockets of his long black coat, parted to reveal a gray vest. A black string tie hung from the white, wilted and dusty collar of his shirt. He strolled along the platform to the far end and looked toward the town. His sharp gray eyes searched along its single street.

His full, uneven lips pressed in a grimace and he turned to look eastward down the tracks. He looked up at the station sign. Black letters proclaimed, EDEN, WYOMING TERRITORY, and a second line below, CHICAGO & FAR WESTERN RAILROAD. He moved slowly along the platform, an eager long-legged stride obviously held in check by necessity. He wanted to get on with his job—his new job.

A slight sound caused him to wheel about, long, angular face alight. A man appeared, stopped short, faded eyes and wrinkled face curious. Gray hair stirred in the steady Wyoming wind. "How-dee. Aim to take the train?"

"West to Warbow. When's it due?"

"Hard to say, what with things like Injuns or a buffalo herd or a washout. Never can tell—"

"I know," the stranger cut in. "Same way down in Kansas."

"From that far, huh?"

"By way of Denver."

"Saw you git off the stage. Aim to catch the train? Hardly anyone does, but she stops here anyhow. Ain't many towns along the line clean to Butte, and crew and passengers like to stretch their legs when they git a chance."

"The train? When's it due?"

"Well, right now for that matter. Might be half

hour or tomorrow—or midnight tonight. Like I said, depends."

"Well . . . whenever, I'll take it."

"Come right inside and get your ticket! Warbow, you say? Heard there's been some Injun trouble out there in Montana."

"So there was. Over now."

"How you know? You just come up from the south."

"You can't tell which way the wind will carry news."

"Now that's a fact! Injuns gone, eh? Blackfoot, we heard here in Eden. Sent a troop of cavalry . . . oh, maybe eight, ten months ago. Reckon they've moved out if the redskins have calmed their feathers."

"I'll find out in Warbow."

"Reckon so. Now about that ticket."

The young man shook his head, reached into an inside pocket of his long coat and produced an object which he extended to the stationmaster. The old man squinted at the square of metal.

"Pass. Chicago & Far Western Railroad. Issued to Lawrence Crane, Supervisor, Land Agents. Land Sales Department. Signed: Jepson Reeves, Vice-President. This pass good at all times and for all accommodations. Charge equivalent fares and expenses authorized by Lawrence Crane to Land Department, Chicago."

The old man studied the stranger with new

interest. He had to look up at the smiling face of the tall young man. He noted the wide shoulders and the deep chest, the raven black hair of the sideburns. About thirty, the old man judged, one of those deceptively slender men who would prove to be all wiry muscle. Handsome devil, too, the stationmaster thought with a touch of envy. That long jaw and wide, smiling lips, those eyes alight with friendliness, the long-planed smooth cheeks would make a woman take a second look.

Crane suddenly turned eastward. The old man saw the smudge of black afar off. "She's coming. You got maybe a half hour or more by the time she gets here, stops, and then takes off westerly. There's a café of sorts in the hotel."

Larry Crane realized he was hungry. He smiled his thanks and followed directions down the street with a long, lithe stride.

It was well beyond a half hour when the coach in which Larry sat jerked as couplings took up slack and slowly Eden, Wyoming Territory, moved back beyond the window and was soon lost to sight and memory. Larry stretched long legs under the seat ahead. Three men and a woman sat in widely spaced seats. The conductor came in from the caboose and extended a hand for Larry's ticket. He looked in surprise at the pass and then with real interest at Larry.

"Where to?"

"Warbow."

"Checking on the land agent there? Word has it there's trouble even after the Indians were chased off. Heard Harvey's all upset about it."

"Harvey? . . . Oh, Gagnle, the land agent. I'll see him." Larry indicated the three other passengers, checking the conductor's curiosity. "Looks like you're not paying for hauling the coach."

"Never do! What's up this way? A town between Eden and Warbow, then nothing to Butte. Beyond that, mountains and so much woods you get sick of looking at fir trees. Then plains. Nothing there to haul until Seattle. C&FW don't make the salary of the train crew on this run."

"You will."

The conductor gave him a sardonic look. "Want to bet?

"Seeing as you're kind of one of us railroaders, come on back to the caboose. We stir up a slumgullion come evening and eggs come morning. Coffee's always on and there's a bunk vacant. Better'n being cramped here."

Larry smiled his thanks and followed the conductor. He met the brakeman, who poured coffee, and the three sat watching the Wyoming plains roll by. After the second cup of coffee, he stretched out on a bunk and closed his eyes. Gradually the click of wheels, the sway of the caboose, lulled Larry, and his thoughts began to move in a half-dream state. He pictured the train as he had seen it coming to the station; funnel-shaped stack on the long and squat locomotive, four boxcars, a flatcar with covered mining machinery for distant Butte, then the passenger coach and the caboose.

What an insignificant string for a trans-continental train from Chicago's lake to Seattle's sound! He recalled the stations along this far northern line of rails of C&FW—plenty through Illinois and in Wisconsin, but spaced farther and farther apart as the rails converged on the Missouri and then followed that mighty stream westward for a time, arcing away and finding its own easy grades on the steady ascent toward the Continental Divide.

Eden to Warbow—over half of Wyoming and deep into Montana. His mind leapt the great distance to Butte. Beyond? As the conductor had said, empty of people, towns, farms, ranches.

The great task of the land agents—build that country up. Make crossroads into villages; villages, towns; towns into cities! Bring men here who would wrest the land's riches for man's use. Bring their families, for women, children and homes represent stability and permanent wealth for any area.

He stirred with a new excitement and a sense he had become more a part of it. Jepson Reeves had said as much in that hotel in Denver, where Larry had suddenly been called from the Kansas plains.

He fixed on that recent memory of the hotel suite a floor below Horace Tabor's ornate quarters. Pale and myopic Bloggett had ushered Larry in and Reeves had extended a pudgy hand and simultaneously dismissed Bloggett. An inner door opened and Harriet Reeves appeared. A single glance confirmed Larry's opinion of many weeks before. She was a beautiful woman, and she knew it.

She swept forward, extending her hand. "Mr. Crane! I was so glad when Uncle said he'd called you to Denver."

"That makes two of us."

She smiled, eyes deepening. Reeves made a soft, impatient sound and his niece instantly understood. "But I'm interfering with business. Shall I see you afterwards?"

"Dinner tonight," Jepson answered shortly for Larry, and Harriet smiled and left. Jepson walked to a cabinet, returned with bottle and glasses. Larry looked on in surprise as he poured two stiff drinks. The little man thrust a glass into Larry's hand. He abruptly asked, "How many land agents do we have?"

"How many? Why . . . hard to say. They're scattered all over the West, from Canada to Mexico and the Gulf."

"That's right—wherever our rails run. And we have a north and south system. We built a lot of railroad ourselves and we've bought up other lines. A western network, C&FW."

Jepson's small body suddenly seemed gigantic. "And we have our own land subsidies, took in those of the roads we bought. Empty land and we have to—" He cut himself short. "But you know that. Point is, will it go smoothly everywhere? Will all sales and all developments work out just as they should?"

Larry chuckled. "I can say from my own experience—no."

"You handled your problems well, and on your own. Think you could handle others?"

"I can try."

"There's a new job in C&FW. Supervisor of all land agents and troubleshooter wherever needed." Reeves lifted his glass in a small salute. "Mr. Lawrence Crane holds it down."

Larry gave a start that caused a dollop of whiskey to splash out of the glass onto his hand. Reeves' smile erased the hard shrewdness about his eyes. He again made a slight salute. "Accept your toast, Larry."

Larry came to his feet, stunned and still unable to speak. He clinked the glass and drank, needing the balancing bite of the whiskey.

Reeves waved him back to his chair. "Sit down. You're much too tall for a vice-president to order about and that's exactly what I intend to do."

Larry rediscovered his voice. "I didn't

expect . . . didn't know . . . Look, I only worked in Kansas and—"

"A man doesn't have to work for me for years before I know what he can do. Things happen and I watch how he handles them. So, you're in the new job."

"Well—I . . . thanks—"

"Wait, Crane! Believe me! You'll earn every cent of your new salary—by the way, that started when you boarded the train for Denver. I'm sending you to Warbow in the Montana Territory. Land agent there is Harvey Gagnle. He's done all right, but the chips never came down until recently. Now—well, you'll see. It's a crazy mix-up of Indians, soldiers, and cowboys."

He crossed the room to a desk and returned with a file which he pushed at Larry. "Here are the reports and letters between Gagnle and the Chicago office. By the way, you'll still have Marlowe there as your boss, but you'll report directly to me, with a copy to Marlowe for Chicago records. Anyhow, go through the file and if you have any questions, I'll be over there at the desk."

Larry turned to the file. The picture rapidly became clear. Warbow range had been purchased and settled by a group of Texans whom the railroad had persuaded to open up far northern spreads. The Indians had been "pacified" by cavalry and there had been no trouble.

Larry followed developments; herds driven up from Texas and set to graze, new ranches following the original few, a town springing up to serve the ranches, under the urging of the railroad. Warbow centered on the logical industry of the country—beef and ranches. The railroad land department had a shrewd eye for what would flourish where.

So far, Harvey Gagnle had done an excellent job. Larry turned to the next report and—Indian marauders, a band of reservation rebels intent on getting a bonus of loot, burning, and rapine. The Army called in through Gagnle's near hysterical telegrams to Marlowe in Chicago. Indians driven off, killed, rounded up and returned to reservation, and all but one cavalry company returned to regimental base in Great Falls. Peace again until . . .

Larry turned to the reports that followed. C Troop, 15th Cavalry Regiment still bivouacked at Warbow. No more Indians, no sign of them, but C Troop remains. Quarrels and fights developing and increasing between troopers, cowboys, townsmen, and Harvey Gagnle reported, in violated dignity, of one episode concerning himself. Larry turned to the next series of letters, telegrams, and reports between Warbow and Chicago.

Women insulted by troopers on the street. Gagnle wrote with prim delicacy to Marlowe, the sentence catching Larry's eye, ". . . expected to certain (I will not call them) 'ladies' who 'entertain' . . ." Larry's scanning eyes sped on. ". . . but daughters and wives of merchants . . . No real law here except a town marshal and he's helpless . . . most influential rancher and commanding officer of C Troop hate one another . . . Now rustling and it just may be the troopers, a hard-drinking, tough lot as I suppose they have to be but . . . I can't do my job efficiently under the circumstances. Please advise quickly. This may get entirely out of hand. No control of cowboys and no authority— even the marshal—over the acts of any man or officer of the U.S. Cavalry . . ."

Larry closed the file. Reeves swung around from the desk. "Well?"

"I earn my raise—starting immediately."

"Can you straighten it up?"

"Texans—U.S. Cavalry—rustling? Warbow's ready for a blowup."

"Well?"

"Direct answer, Mr. Reeves. I can try . . . that is if it hasn't blown sky-high already."

Reeves studied him, blue eyes hard and searching, and then he smiled. "Then we have no more business to discuss. Enjoy as much of Denver as you can today and we'll have dinner tonight. Bloggett will have your stage ticket north and your permanent railroad pass ready. You'll leave in the morning."

And so he had, Larry thought, stretched out on the bunk in the swaying caboose. He had left with the memory of the hotel's ornate dining room, of excellent food and good wine and cigars. He had the memory of the silver-lode kings and their bejeweled ladies, none of whom touched Harriet Reeves in beauty. He had left with the memory of her warm hand in his at parting and of her wry smile and voice.

"We fairly dart across one another's paths, don't we? A hello and an immediate good-bye, first one place and then another."

"Your uncle keeps me busy."

She gently disengaged her hand. "Perhaps sometime I might persuade Uncle Jep to allow our paths to parallel instead of crossing. Good night and good luck."

Even as his memory faded into full sleep, Larry gave a small sigh, turned on the bunk, and surrendered to the lulling rhythm of the clicking wheels.

Chapter II

Sometime in the night the train entered Montana and sped heedlessly on. Larry catnapped, ate, played pinochle with crewmen, slept again, and the train moved steadily on through another night. Mid-morning of the next day, Larry felt the train slow and heard the blasting whistle of the locomotive. He picked up his carpetbag and stepped out on the rear platform. He could see only rolling swales, like waves eternally frozen in mid-motion.

The caboose jerked as the train slowed again. Slowly Warbow came into view; a scattering of empty cattle pens and the squat orange and black station cut off the view of the town's single street of false-fronted stores and buildings.

The train came to a final jerk and stop. Larry saw the dark blue uniform and the single gold chevron on the sleeve of a loafing cavalryman, then caught the surprised but bold eyes of a woman obviously from the local saloon and dance hall. Larry swung off the step onto the platform. Then he saw the little knot of cowboys up toward the locomotive. He searched the small group for the land agent, Gagnle.

His roving glance held on a petite figure in summery white, pert face shaded by a small parasol. She wore lacy gloves on dainty hands and a little bonnet sat at an eye-catching angle on a mass of honey-gold curls. She looked as though she did not belong in this grim Montana setting.

Just then she looked his way and he gazed into cornflower-blue eyes that widened slightly and then lowered demurely as her small, vivid lips made the faintest of smiles.

The train whistle shattered the skies. Couplings took up slack with a clang and the train moved slowly, picked up speed, and rolled away westward. The girl with the parasol came down the short platform toward Larry. He stepped aside as she passed, slanting a covert bright blue gleam of eyes at him.

Larry turned to the stationmaster but swung around when he heard, "Now ain't you something to look at, m'am!"

The trooper had pushed away from the station wall. He stood tall and heavyset, sweeping moustache accenting the coarse lines of his cheeks and jaw. He grinned with insulting wisdom. The girl's head came up proudly and she gathered in her skirt as though contact with the soldier would soil it, and swept by him like a haughty princess.

Larry heard quickening steps behind him as the trooper swaggered after the girl as she turned the corner of the station. The cowboys hurried by. They looked grim and they moved with long, determined strides that rang an alarm bell along Larry's nerves.

The stationmaster regained his voice. "This could tear up the town again."

Larry strode after the punchers. When he stepped clear of the station, he had an instant view along the length of Warbow's street, this end of it opening on fifty yards or so of packed, barren ground.

The girl with the parasol had covered half of it in her dignified retreat. Just behind her strolled the trooper, unaware of the cowboys, who had increased their pace. The trooper came up beside the girl. She swung angrily around. Larry could not quite distinguish her words, but her voice came angry and curt. The trooper threw back his head and gave a loud, mocking laugh.

The punchers came up. Larry saw the soldier, laugh choked back, swing sharply around as the punchers converged on him. Larry saw fists swing. The girl screamed and raced toward the street. The fighting mass heaved, suddenly parted. The trooper, hat knocked off, lips bleeding, stood at bay. His roaring voice called, "C Troop! C Troop!"

The cowboys converged on him again and he disappeared. Larry stood hesitant. He didn't like the odds against the single man and yet the soldier had brought it on himself. Sudden, angry shouts along the distant street brought Larry's sharp eyes away from the fight. He saw blue-clad figures erupt from a saloon, and more from another building farther down the street. They raced toward the fight.

The girl with the parasol, fleeing from the fight, suddenly flung herself aside to press against a wall as soldiers streamed by her. Larry saw town citizens and cowboys suddenly burst into the street and run after the rescuing troopers. The original melee roiled and boiled in the dust of the station area. The moustached trooper's dark body literally catapulted out and down. Larry could almost hear the thud as he struck the packed earth. Larry saw the flash of a boot and the trooper, half rising, fell back as a heavy leather toe caught him in the side.

Now the other cavalrymen threw themselves into the melee and the mob broke up into little sections of fighting, cursing men. A moment later the rest of the town fell on the troopers. Men cursed, fists lashed, and kicking boots thudded against bodies. This was riot!

A Colt blasted and thundered. Now bullets would fly and—Larry checked the thought as the gun roared again and a man with a bright star on his dark shirt fired the gun a third time over the fighting groups. Citizen and soldier swung around to face this new threat.

The lawman held his Colt, hammer dogged

back, muzzle uptilted but ready to drop and spit flame. "This has gone far enough. Do any of you know what you're fighting about?"

The moustached trooper lay unmoving, a puncher with fists ready standing almost over him but watching the lawman. The silence held a long tense moment until the stationmaster called, "Ralph! Marshal Banks! It was that one—he caused it."

He indicated the cavalryman who suddenly sat up, bloody head dangling and arms limp. The stationmaster hurried on. "He insulted Miss Carrie and some Rocking K hands—"

"That's right," the cowboy near the trooper blazed. "He stopped Miss Carrie. She can tell you."

The lawman's slow gaze moved around the crowd, then rested on Larry. Larry felt the impact of steady, penetrating eyes and then they moved on. He asked of both stationmaster and puncher: "Witnesses?"

"Why"—the stationmaster swung and pointed —"him—he just got off the train."

Again brown eyes met Larry's and the marshal shot a silent question across the space between them. Larry reluctantly walked forward, accidentally enmeshed in a situation before he was prepared for it. "Is that so, mister?" the lawman demanded.

"I didn't hear what the soldier said to the lady,

so I can't swear to insult. But he did go after and stop her."

"It was insult, friend, depend on it." The lawman wheeled around. "All right, scatter! Get on down the street. I'll bend this gun barrel over the head of anyone who starts anything. Understand? . . . Now, go on! Move out!"

"What about him?" the puncher indicated the groggy trooper at his feet.

"He cools off in jail. Go on, move out!"

Slowly, the men started drifting away to the street. Now and then, they would look back as though hunting reason to fight again. The lawman realized that the soldiers had not moved off but had imperceptibly bunched. He glared at them. "You heard me. Get about your business."

One soldier flung a challenge. "You can't order us to do a damn thing."

"Soldier, if my badge means nothing, maybe a peacemaker does."

The trooper stood uncertain. Suddenly his eyes cut away, then widened with pleased surprise. He snapped erect and his voice bawled. "Attention!"

A man came striding up. Larry recognized the golden emblem on the dark blue, broad-brimmed campaign hat and the double gold bars of a captain on the broad shoulders. The officer's face was deep tanned with little crowfeet of sun and distance about black, prideful eyes. His nose had a flaunting hawklike arch and his bloodless lips under a thin moustache had set in an expression of anger and distaste.

"At ease, men."

He came to parade-ground halt before the lawman, glanced at the fallen trooper who now looked around out of swollen eyes. The captain's mouth turned into a pale, bloodless line. He spoke over his shoulder: "Ingram, what happened to Murphy?"

The marshal said, "I can tell you—"

"You were not asked, Marshal. Well, Ingram?"

The trooper who had challenged the lawman said, "A bunch of cowboys beat him up, sir. We tried to help but—"

"I watched from the hotel porch, Ingram. I could see what happened."

"Yes, sir. And then Marshal Banks—"

"I also saw what Marshal Banks did, Ingram." The captain faced the lawman directly. Larry detected the subtle signs of the irritable martinet in the officer's proper stance, cold voice, and unyielding eyes. "I thank you for helping my men, sir, though they would have taken care of the matter."

Banks exploded. "My town is in the middle of a riot and—"

"Nonsense, sir! The altercation would swiftly have ended if busybodies—" His voice held disdain. "But we have an old argument again. I'll not get into it."

He turned on his heel to face his men. "Dismissed! Ingram, take Murphy back to the post."

"Captain Darnell," the marshal snapped, "that man insulted Carrie Keiler. He started this fight. He'll pay a fine or go to jail."

Darnell swung about, his face suffused with dark anger and violated authority. He glared down his hawk nose. "I am sorry the lovely Miss Keiler was insulted. Convey my apologies. But also convey my advice to Mr. Keiler to keep his daughter away from places where she invites honest male admiration. The young lady is too much aware of her charms, sir. Blame that rather than Trooper Murphy."

His voice changed to a commanding growl. "Let me remind you, Marshal Banks, your authority—such as it is—is confined to Warbow and its citizens. My men are not subject to it. We are subject to military, not civilian law. My patience runs thin, sir."

"Like me, Captain, your job is to make peace—"

"And I shall keep it, not only among raiding Indians but also belligerent civilians. I am empowered to order martial law. I don't want to, but if C Troop's enforced stay in this God-forsaken excuse for a town leads to constant harassment, that is exactly what I will do. My troopers have the run of this town, when on pass or liberty, sir."

His black, imperious eyes held the marshal as his thin lips moved in an order. "Ingram! Return Murphy to the post. Put him in dispensary for checkup."

He stood solid and challenging as his men jumped to help Murphy to his feet. Larry watched Marshal Banks. The lawman stood with his fists clenched. He followed the troopers with his eyes. When they had gone, he said, "Darnell—"

"Captain, sir! That is my rank."

Banks choked out, "Captain, you'll push this military thing too far. How long do you think we'll stand for drunken soldiers like—"

"As long as C Troop is here. I hope that won't be long, sir. Orders moving my command would be like a heavenly trumpet."

He started to turn, and was checked as he saw Larry. "You, sir, are new?"

"That's right, Captain. Just stepped off the train."

Darnell's lips curled. "Welcome to Warbow, sir. That's purely rhetorical, believe me. Accept my wish that your business won't hold you too long. Good day, sir."

He smiled thinly and Larry could only nod. The officer turned on his heel and strode away at march step. Larry and the marshal, alone on the bare, boot-churned ground, watched him go.

The marshal spoke through tight-clenched teeth. "Just get on down the street, friend, and leave me alone."

Larry picked up his carpetbag and walked away. Up ahead, he saw troopers lifting Murphy into a military vehicle. The driver snapped his whip and the wagon rolled quickly away down the street, iron tires kicking up dust.

The first building, near the tracks, was a saloon and a woman stood on its porch, eyeing Larry as he walked by. He saw on either side the usual cow-town range of business ventures, from barbershop to saddlery. Gray eyes stabbing into store windows, doorways, and saloon porches, Larry saw no soldiers. If they hadn't all left, they held themselves discreetly within some gambling hall or saloon, he decided.

He came to a small structure just this side of the hotel and read the gilded lettering on the small window. "Land Office, Chicago & Far Western Railroad—Harvey Gagnle, Agent."

Larry had a momentary stab of nostalgia for Kansas. Then he saw a round, frightened face peering from a corner of the window. Larry changed course and walked in.

A sweeping look took in the cubbyhole of an office, familiar from battered desk to the survey map on the wall, though it had more red "sold" area than Larry had colored. The man at the window had wheeled around and asked, "Yes, sir? Can I help you?"

"You're Mr. Gagnle, the agent?"

"That's right. You were down at the station? What happened?"

Larry dropped his carpetbag to the floor. He had an impression of a man half a foot shorter than himself, with thick body, rounded face, and frightened eyes. Soft, Larry thought, all right until—he recalled Reeves' phrase—"the chips are down."

"A brawl between soldiers and townsmen, I'd say."

Gagnle ran fleshy fingers distractedly through thin, dark red hair. "Unusual. Doesn't often happen. Warbow is peaceful and progressive. I'm sorry that you saw it, sir. You needn't think that Warbow—"

"I'm not a land buyer, Gagnle."

"No? Then . . . ?"

Larry opened the carpetbag, took out an envelope and extended it to Gagnle. The man turned it over several times. He gave Larry an underbrow look and then pulled out the brief letter from Jepson Reeves.

He scanned the concise introduction and orders. Larry could see relief pour through the man. He looked up, round eyes alight with new hope. He extended his hand. "Mr. Crane! They sent you! Thank God you've come!"

Larry accepted the soft clasp and looked out through the window onto Warbow's street. He smiled crookedly. "Rather thank the devil, Mr. Gagnle, from what I've just seen. And I'm not too sure I'll thank him."

Chapter III

Larry sat in a chair and Gagnle darted to the desk, pulled open the deep lower drawer and took out a bottle and glasses. He explained as he hastily poured, spilling a little, "Am I glad you've come!"

Larry accepted the glass and Gagnle uncomfortably shifted weight from one leg to the other. Larry said, "Sit down and be comfortable. It's your office."

"But you're my boss, I reckon. And—" He dropped into the chair. "Thank you."

Larry checked a faint frown at the man's revealing nervousness and looked around the office again and then up at the sales-survey map. "From the red, looks like you've sold a lot of railroad land, Gagnle. Or can I say Harvey?"

"Please make it Harve." Gagnle also looked at the map. "I didn't personally sell all that—direct, that is. Chicago office brought up some Texas ranchers and I showed them around. But the deal was main office."

"How long have you been in Warbow?"

"Right from the beginning! I came out with the crew that surveyed the government grants to C&FW. Lived in tents and kept rifles and Colts handy in case of the Blackfeet. After the survey, I

31

worked out of the station. Sold the first lot in Warbow itself to Richards for his general store . . . just down the street."

"Good start, Harve. Warbow is on railroad land?"

"That's right. All up and down the street and the houses beyond, either side—I made the deals."

Larry deliberately wheeled about to face the map. "A lot more land to be sold and a lot more to be done to develop the town and area. What happened?"

"It's not my fault, Mr. Crane."

"Tell me about it."

Gagnle sighed and lifted the bottle, but Larry shook his head. Regretfully, Gagnle left his glass empty and slowly started to talk. He told the story of Warbow essentially as Larry had read it in the folder back in Denver. He told of the need to call in the cavalry when the Indian renegades broke out of the reservation.

"They sent C Troop," Gagnle said, "and Captain Darnell moved fast and struck hard. Those Indians were damn glad to get back where they belonged."

"C Troop is still here."

"That's the cause of all the trouble. Will you tell me, Mr. Crane, why they weren't sent back to their regiment long ago?"

"I've known the Army to do wonders—in reverse sometimes. I could guess, but that's about all. When you asked for help against the Indians, where did you send the request?"

"Well, Ralph Banks, he's the marshal, Fred Keiler and his friends and me sent it to the War Department."

"Washington! Some bright young desk officer looked at a map, made up an order detaching C Troop for duty here and that was that."

"But why haven't they gone back! Here they stay."

"The bright young officer forgot probably. So, since Washington sent C Troop, only Washington can order them back to regular duty. They've been forgotten."

Gagnle absorbed the information. "But—but Ralph Banks and Keiler sent a blistering letter to Washington, demanding C Troop's withdrawal!"

"I'm just guessing from what I learned in Virginia, Tennessee, and Georgia. Wartime then, of course, but not now. Promotions in rank are slow with the Army reduced to nothing."

"What has that to do with it?"

"Might be the answer if my guess is right. The bright young lieutenant forgot to keep in touch with Darnell's reports. A blunder with no excuse."

"That it is!"

"So our young officer just sent your request to burial in the files."

"But he could *order* C Troop—"

"Not at all. It took a general to send C Troop and it'll take a general—in Washington—to move 'em again. Our young man knows if he's caught in a blunder like this, he could lose file points. So . . . he hopes it's not brought to light before he gets a promotion or a transfer. Let the next bright desk officer with a single gold bar take the rap."

"But look what's happening to us!"

"What has happened?"

"Townsmen and troopers ready to fight one another any time and any place. Those troopers know they can't be touched. So they do things that'd put me or you in jail in a flash."

"Like talking to Miss Keiler?"

"That's not the only trouble, Mr. Crane. There's rustling. A lot of suspicion is on the soldiers."

"That's ridiculous!"

"Not that I'm arguing, Mr. Crane, but do you know what a plain soldier's pay is? Twelve dollars a month—and a sergeant twenty-one! That's what they tell me. Here they sit with nothing to do but drink, gamble, and fool around with girls like Vera or Goldie at the Branding Iron. Time on their hands and Captain Darnell wouldn't listen to any complaint against his men. He hates Warbow civilians. So, why not rustle a few head of beef now and then?"

"No answer . . . yet."

"Another thing, Mr. Crane. Fred Keiler is kingpin. He headed the first bunch of Texans that came up here. Do you think a man comes to me, the land agent, to find out where he can set up a spread? Not on your life! He goes to Fred Keiler! Why, Fred has even vetoed a sale I've made, sending the jasper to homestead land clean to hell and gone away from Warbow. If it hadn't been for C&FW Keiler wouldn't even be here! It's not fair."

"That's the railroad's viewpoint, Harve, not his."

"All right, maybe I'm too much a railroad man! So forget that angle. But I was leading up to another bit of trouble. There's Keiler and you can see what kind of man he must be. There's Captain Darnell and—you saw him today."

"I saw him—and heard him."

"So you figure what happens when Keiler and Darnell hate one another. Keiler figures to rule Warbow his way and Darnell his. Keiler hates soldiers and Darnell hates punchers. Between the two of them the town's torn apart."

Gagnle jumped up in distress and paced across the office. He stopped short, looking out the window, and said in a low voice, "Mr. Crane, come here. Hurry!"

Gagnle pointed out the window. "See them? Miss Carrie and the man?"

He saw the girl with the white dress and parasol strolling along the far walk. A tall man walked beside her, a man who wore gunbelt and Colt, scarred boots, broken brimmed puncher's hat and faded Levi's.

"That's Matt Arnold, Mr. Crane. He ramrods Rocking K for Fred Keiler. Nothing he likes better'n a barroom brawl, and I've heard a dozen different people say he's fast as lightning with that gun he wears."

Larry had a glimpse of a long, lean face, tanned and angular. He saw an irregular mouth flash a grin as sharp and swift as a steel trap. Larry had the impression of a handsome, ruthless animal, as the man strolled on with Carrie Keiler.

Gagnle turned from the window. "If it wasn't for Matt Arnold, Keiler wouldn't be half the man he thinks he is. Matt came up from Texas with the first Rocking K trail herd and they must have raised him on rattlesnakes down there."

Larry dropped back into his chair. "It takes a tough man to drive a trail herd and to run a ranch as big as Rocking K must be."

"That he is! You should see the bar girls get flustered! So do town girls, but they don't have a chance."

"You mean to say the bar girls—"

"Not that! Matt has his eye on Carrie Keiler and there's every chance he might be Rocking K's owner some day."

"Good to know this, Harve, but where does it fit in?"

"Where! That man has beat up three troopers and he'd like nothing better than to start a fight. He keeps every rancher and puncher in the area scared of Keiler and Rocking K so that when Keiler speaks, everyone jumps."

Larry steepled long fingers to his lips as he frowned out the window. Gagnle sighed. "So anyone comes to Warbow for business or a ranch won't have a thing to do with it when they learn what's going on. Five prospects just up and run in the past two weeks, Mr. Crane. Any wonder I asked for help? I'm glad you're going to take over for a while."

Larry's head came up. "Harve, you have the wrong idea. You're land agent and this is still your problem."

Gagnle's round face grew lugubrious. He blinked and then spread his hands in a helpless gesture. "But—but, then . . . what are you going to do?"

Larry picked up the carpetbag. "First, I'm going to the hotel, get a bath and a good meal. Then I'll have a drink here and there and talk to anyone willing to."

"But I've told you everything—"

"You've been a big help. But might be I'll pick up something else."

"I don't miss much."

"I'd like to talk to a soldier, if they haven't all left—and maybe a Rocking K hand, or a puncher from most any ranch." Larry placed his hat on his head. "Then I'll ride around and talk some more." He lightly dropped his hand on Gagnle's soft broad shoulder. "We just might come up with some answer between us. Or maybe no answer at all to the tangled rope you have here. Oh, and Harve, if anyone asks, just say I'm inspecting railroad property—like the station and the loading pens. Nothing about land, huh?"

Gagnle looked puzzled but nodded.

Larry walked slowly toward the hotel. He wasn't quite sure why he had given the last instruction to Gagnle except for an instinctive hunch he didn't want Warbow to associate him too closely with the land agent, who might not measure up to the rough standards of the town. In fact, he hadn't quite measured up to Larry's.

He only half noted the surrey at the hitch-rack as he turned into the hotel. But, as he placed a boot on the first step, two men and the blonde in white came out. Larry identified Carrie Keiler and Matt Arnold. The second man, though taller than Jepson Reeves, had much the same prideful walk and arrogant set of the head. He had a thin, age-leathered face with a white moustache as imperious as his eyes.

Larry stepped aside to let them pass. The girl's cornflower-blue eyes met his. Larry removed his hat with a slight bow. Matt Arnold's stride broke and eyes, black as an Indian's and just as cruel, flamed at him.

The trio passed and Arnold helped the girl into the surrey as the old man circled to the driver's seat. Larry heard Arnold's harsh voice. "Who was that?"

"I haven't the faintest idea. I saw him get off the train. And who cares who he is?"

Larry moved up the stairs. Now *there* was a comment on the importance of Lawrence Crane!

Chapter IV

At the hotel, the café, and two saloons, Larry confirmed Gagnle's general statements of the situation. Animosity was high against the soldiers, but he had no chance to hear a trooper's side, for he did not encounter one anywhere.

Warbow was quickly explored afoot from the northern outskirts to the stock pens that bound it to the south. Larry returned by way of the station and once more strolled along the single business street.

He came to the marshal's office and small, sturdy jail. The office was small, plain walls relieved only by reward dodgers, a locked rifle case and a row of coathooks just behind the single, scarred desk. Just beyond, a barred door, open now, led to a short cell block.

Larry called, "Marshal?" No one answered. He saw a chair under one of the street windows and he sat down. He scanned the reward notices, some of them curling and yellowing with age. He pulled out his watch, replaced it, and stood up. Just then the marshal suddenly filled the door. Larry swung around as the lawman sharply eyed him. "Have you been waiting long?"

"Not long and it doesn't matter."

The marshal circled his desk and dropped into

the chair behind it. "I remember you—down at the station during that fight."

"That's right."

"You've got trouble of some kind?"

"No more than the rest of Warbow, from what I've heard here and there about the town."

"Talk's cheap around here."

"And fights a'plenty. More bound to come, they tell me. Sooner or later someone will get killed. Maybe we can find something we can do about it, you and me."

Banks held his gaze level and inscrutable. "For a stranger, just come, you're bleeding a bit too much about our town."

Larry produced a card from his pocket and dropped it on the desk. Banks placed it precisely before him. Larry said, "I have an interest in Warbow. It's part of my job and that's something I don't want to lose."

"You and Harve Gagnle—?"

"He's local. I'm out of Chicago, a trouble-shooter in this case. I've about got the whole picture, except for what the merchants might say."

"Most of 'em would say if C Troop left, they'd lose business. Captain Darnell requisitions food, staples, and supplies locally. The saloons like the troopers better'n punchers. Some of 'em in town every night on liberty, while the punchers work all week and drink and kick their heels come

Saturday. That's from the business side, though."

"There's another side?"

"The kind of thing you saw today. A brawl started right in Richard's store. Hal Prins' saloon got chairs and tables smashed and lost a heap of glassware. So everybody wants it to end."

"Except the cowboys and the soldiers."

"I ain't so sure. Would you look forward to a broken jaw or smashed face as part of a night off from work?"

"I've heard a lot about rustling. True?"

"Steady little dribbles here and there, but enough I know I got to stop it fast."

"Soldiers?"

Banks made a grimace. "You've heard that. It could be, but I've had no more proof of it than wild guesses when some rancher was mad when his beef was hit."

"No leads? No trails?"

"If there was, the rustling would be over, friend." Banks sighed. "Now that we've talked, what more do you think you can do?"

"You're the law and I wouldn't do a thing without you behind me. The railroad wants to sell its land. I'm just authorized to tell you the railroad will back you and it's ready to help if you need it. I'll be around a while."

After a long moment, Banks said, "You can help right now. No one in Warbow can talk sense to Darnell. And same goes for Keiler. The captain

42

figures we're lousy civilians and deserve nothing. Keiler figures we don't come from Texas and deserve nothing. But you're a stranger and maybe they'll listen to you."

"What can I tell 'em?"

"It'd be Keiler first, I reckon. The railroad still has range him and his Texan friends want. Might be you could hint the railroad . . ."

Larry finished for him. ". . . won't sell to Texans anymore?"

"Unless he calls off his feud with Darnell. Then, with that promise, you could go to Darnell. He'd listen, what with your railroad authority. Not that it'd affect him, but he'd figure you could hold things in line."

"Now that's a program, Marshal. All based on guess and bluff. If you think it will work . . ."

"It's worth a try. Anything is, to get peace on this range. Then I could put all my mind to those rustlers."

Larry stood up. "How do I get to Rocking K?"

Banks gave explicit directions and the next morning, Larry rode out of Warbow on a rangy but powerful black gelding. This northern country was deceptive, and he became quite aware of it as he rode alone into the heart of it. He had the impression of great unbroken space, of a sea of grass broken only by low bushes and here and there a tree, flowing under a great bowl of a sky. But there were great wide and deep swales into which he would descend and he had the impression that low hills rose before and behind him until the road climbed the next slope and once more his vision seemed unobstructed.

Deep in one of these swales, he suddenly heard the rattle of metal and a rumble of hoofs. At the same moment, the gelding's ears pointed forward. Without warning, riders appeared at the crest of the road above, moving with a precision that Larry recognized instantly.

Each rider stood silhouetted against the bright sky for an instant and then came down the slope. Larry pulled aside as the eight troopers passed, led by one with a corporal's chevrons. Each man gave him a sidelong glance as he passed, but there was no other sign of recognition. Dust billowed up and around Larry and then the troopers climbed the far slope and disappeared in the direction of Warbow.

It had happened so swiftly and without warning that Larry suddenly had the key to a thing that had bothered him. He had wondered how rustlers could operate without more than the usual risk of detection. Now he knew.

A few miles farther, he topped a ridge and drew rein. He looked down on a small valley. A stream wound through it and, clustered about it just below, were the buildings of C Troop. He eased back in the saddle and watched the activities. The camp looked permanent, until he realized that the buildings were all jerrybuilt, a temporary base from which the troop could campaign against the Indians and return for rest between forays. As he watched, a squad of eight rode out on the far side of the camp, splashing across the stream and continuing north. Obviously Captain Darnell still sent out patrols even though the Indians were gone.

A good officer, at least, Larry thought, keeping to camp routine, patrols working off some of the steam men accumulate who are forced to remain in one place without visible or logical reason.

But it was not enough, Larry thought, as he turned back down the slope and followed it eastward toward Rocking K. This was not the cavalry Larry had known in his four years of service, where eager young men fought for either the Stars and Stripes or the Stars and Bars. Reduced sadly in number, with low pay and slow promotion, the men were the scourings and misfits of the cities, towns, and farms. They had been whipped by rigid discipline into tough fighting cadres, sent to these Indian wars and troubled territories of the West. They were professionals now, imbued with an esprit de corps for their units and for the Army as a whole. But, below this surface, lay savage attitudes. No wonder C Troop set Warbow on edge.

Larry turned the horse slightly toward the south, this time crossing the rolling dips rather than following them. Some distance farther along, he came on grazing beef, all bearing the Rocking K brand. Reassured, Larry rode on without hurry. He rode up a slope as three riders suddenly burst over the crest. Larry instantly recognized one as the foreman, Matt Arnold, who spurred down the slope toward Larry, his two punchers following. He drew rein and cuffed back his hat from his arrogant, dark face. "What are you doing here?"

"Heading to Rocking K."

This close, Larry could more clearly see the signs of cruelty in the faint curl of the lips as Arnold spoke. "You were in town yesterday."

"That's right. Just arrived."

"You sure take a roundabout way to Rocking K if you rode out of Warbow."

"I wanted to see the cavalry post."

Arnold's voice held a soft but dangerous drawl. "And did you talk to our friend, the captain?"

"Not him. I just looked and rode off. My main business is with Mr. Keiler."

"Just him?"

"Of course. No one else owns Rocking K."

Arnold sat a moment. "I'm foreman. I do the hiring, firing, and most of the buying and selling. Maybe you can deal with me."

"Be glad to, Mr. . . . ?"

"Arnold, Matt Arnold."

". . . Mr. Arnold, but I'm not looking for work. I don't want to buy anything or sell you something. No, just Mr. Keiler."

"Ed likes to know who he's seeing and so do I. Who are you and where you from?"

"Lawrence Crane, from Denver; before that Kansas and Chicago. I'm with the Chicago and Far Western. I think your boss would want to see me."

Arnold spoke a word to the two men that sent them on to their work and he reined about. "I'll ride you in, Crane."

After a while Arnold mused aloud, "From the railroad? You hooked up with that paleface land agent, Gagnle?"

"We work for the same company, if that's what you mean."

"Tight-mouthed, ain't you?"

Larry chuckled. "It works out best that way, doesn't it?"

Arnold fell silent and they rode on. They crested a rise and looked down on another small valley, wholly taken up by Rocking K, the ranch house, outbuildings, pens and corrals. Larry involuntarily drew rein and whistled.

Arnold smiled, a peel of thin lips from sharp white teeth. "That's right, Crane. She's big. Big as the one we have down in Texas and kingpin around Warbow."

"I believe you."

Arnold urged his horse down the slope and Larry followed. They threaded between pens, corrals, and buildings for a long time before they moved out into a wide expanse of grass surrounding the main house itself.

As they did, a slim, lovely figure in a light gray cotton dress moved obliquely toward the house from a complex of chicken houses and wire pens. Sunlight gleamed from honey-colored hair that hung loosely down her back, caught at the nape of the neck by a small blue bow. Larry felt Arnold's hard, suspicious eyes on him, and he asked casually, "Who's that?"

"Miss Keiler, Ed's daughter. You ought to know."

"That's right! You were with her at the hotel. Was the man Keiler?"

Arnold looked less suspicious and, paying no attention to the girl, swung out of the saddle. Larry followed and when he straightened and turned, the girl had changed direction and now walked toward them. The light dress clung to her breasts and legs and Larry tried hard not to drink in the lovely, womanly picture. He could almost feel Arnold's harsh suspicion and jealousy.

"A visitor, Matt?" she asked.

"Named Crane, Carrie. From the railroad. Wants to see Ed—on business." Arnold accented the last words as his eyes stayed on Larry.

The girl extended her hand. Her arms were bare almost to the shoulder, tanned and golden. The V of her dress was deep and Larry refused to look at the faint beginning of shadow. But he found her face just as distracting.

"Welcome to Rocking K, Mr. Crane. I'll take you to Father. Thanks, Matt."

The foreman frowned, wanted to object but could find no way. He finally gave a curt nod, glared at Larry, and said, "I'll head you toward Warbow—the direct way—when your business is done."

"This way, Mr. Crane." Carrie turned and threw him a smile over her shoulder. In a split second her eyes deepened to soft violet, both appraising and inviting. She moved a step ahead, walking gracefully with a swing of small hips and wide skirt.

Larry thought she could no more help flirt than breathe. He had sensed the same quality in her yesterday on the station platform and again on the hotel steps. He sensed Arnold behind them, standing and watching by the horses. Larry felt he was on the point of making his first enemy in Warbow.

Chapter V

Once they had rounded a corner and Matt Arnold's eyes could no longer bore into their backs, Carrie abandoned her short lead and dropped back to his side. The crown of her golden head came to the level of his eyes and she looked up at him with a friendly, pert expression. "I remember you at the station, Mr. Crane. I hope the trouble yesterday didn't give you bad thoughts about Warbow."

"Not too bad, m'am, considering our meetings —however brief."

Her eyes glowed, deepened to violet, a change that fascinated Larry. "I'm glad, Mr. Crane. Rocking K seldom sees a stranger."

"Mr. Arnold doesn't like 'em."

"Oh, Matt!" she exclaimed with a curl of lips. "That's tough Texan for you, something like Father."

"That's bad. I'd hope someone—"

Her laugh cut him short and again she gave him a provocative smile and underlash look. "Father's all growl, Mr. Crane, but seldom bites. For my part—and speaking for him—you're welcome any time."

A few moments later, Larry extended his hand to a man no taller than Jepson Reeves, but one all whang-leather, gristle, and once wiry muscles. Keiler looked up at him with the small man's dislike of the tall. Keiler puffed dark lips under his moustache and snapped, "Railroad man. Land agent, like that soft-talking Gagnle."

"Land department," Larry softly corrected, "not agent. I'm out of the Chicago office—Gagnle's boss, you might say."

"Oh? Well, then, you can stop selling land and ship that spineless cub out of here."

Larry's smile remained. "I'd like to hear your thoughts on it—and a few other things, Mr. Keiler. I know there's nothing goes on around here that gets away from you."

Keiler rocked on heel and toe, puffed through his moustache and barked, "Sit down, Crane. Carrie, bring the whiskey bottle and leave it."

Larry took the big leather chair Keiler indicated. He appreciatively followed Carrie's rhythmic walk across the huge room to a cabinet. He looked around as Keiler sat down near him and the old man allowed his guest to absorb the room, the heavy but good furnishings, the lace curtains, and the heavy drapes that could shut out all light.

Carrie brought the bottle and glasses, put them on a table beside her father's hand. She said, "Will you be staying long, Mr. Crane? You're mighty welcome."

"I wish I could but I have to get back to Warbow."

She pouted prettily. "Persuade him if you can, Father."

"We'll see—we'll see. Now if you'll let us talk business . . ."

She gave Larry a long, soft smile and walked gracefully through a rear door and disappeared. Keiler brought Larry's eyes back to him with an abrupt, "What do you think of Rocking K?"

"It's the largest ranch I've ever seen, not only up here, but in Kansas, Colorado, and Wyoming."

"Give you railroad people credit for two things, Crane. You know good ranch land when you see it and you know the right man to tell about it."

"I'd like to hear how you built this up in so few years, sir."

Keiler, pleased, launched into an autobiography. Like many small men, he had felt the need to conquer a tall man's world—and had done it in his way. Yet Larry sensed a loyalty in the man to those who served him without question, to those close to him, like Carrie or a wife whom Larry assumed to be dead before the move up from Texas. Keiler's leathery face grew animated. Once, he even slapped Larry's knee as he laughed, telling of a sharp deal. "So that's the way she was done. And"—he lifted a gnarled finger—"and your railroad can thank me for bringing up my neighbors from down in Texas to buy your land."

"But some, I understand, you sent north to

homestead land. We would have appreciated those sales, sir."

Keiler grunted with a puff of lips. "Baling-wire outfits, Crane, sort of Texas poor relations. Not the kind you'd give a mortgage to. Still, Texans, and that's what I'd like to see up here."

"One good thing we like, sir, a man like you whom we feel on our side and to whom the people up here turn."

"That they do, Crane. Not that I'm boasting, but they trust me here. I reckon I *am* a kind of kingpin advisor."

"I see there's cavalry still here. I thought they'd leave after the Indian trouble."

Keiler exploded into oaths. "Yankees! Every damn one of 'em! And—but maybe you . . . ?"

"Virginia Cavalry, four years, sir."

"Well, then you know what a blue uniform does to me. The worst of those blithering, idiotic Yanks is that Captain Darnell. Seeing him as an officer, I wonder how the Confederacy lost the War!"

"There were probably better officers then, sir. I like to believe so." Larry spoke carefully. "I gather C Troop will be ordered out."

"Like hell! They'll be here forever." Keiler's leathery face suffused. "That is, unless things get pretty tight for Darnell. And they can be! Darnell will find he can't order people around. His soldiers won't have a good time anymore in

Warbow. That troop will stay in camp and rot until they're moved or I give the word."

"Mr. Keiler, I'm quite sure that the railroad wants no more trouble between soldiers and civilians. Why not let things turn peaceful, live with it, until—"

"The railroad wants no trouble! Do I have a hint of pressure there, sir?"

"Not at all. We just ask your cooperation until, between us, we can find some answer to the problem."

"I handle this my way, sir. And should I wait while those soldiers steal my cattle? They've done that! And from other ranchers!"

Larry smiled placatingly. "We'd appreciate it if you would wait, sir. We have more range land to sell, as you know. Knowing your preference, we could hold off, saving it for your friends . . . that is, if you'd go along with us."

Keiler glared, puffed his moustache. "Your land agent here won't sell an inch of land without my approval, sir. He daren't."

"Mr. Gagnle is being considerate. The land department likes that and it could continue. Depends."

Keiler stood up. "Crane, I like you but damned if I like what you're saying."

"I work for the Chicago and Far Western. I hope you like us both. We're not unreasonable, are we?"

Keiler said evasively, "I'll think it over, sir, though I warn you I seldom change my mind. My people listen to me and do what I say. Better'n a damn Yank soldier trying to order 'em around. I'll see you in town?"

"I'd be glad to come out here and save you the trip."

Keiler glanced toward the door through which his daughter had disappeared and answered dryly, "I imagine. Many would. We'll see. Matt Arnold will set you on the Warbow road."

Larry, a messenger dismissed from the court of a king, could only walk out on the porch. Keiler shouted for Arnold who instantly appeared from around a corner of the house. The man shot a look at Larry and then toward the door as though expecting to see Carrie.

Keiler unbent long enough to turn to Larry and, surprisingly, held out his hand. "Crane, you're all right. I'm not sure of your damn railroad. Until then . . ."

"I understand. I hope this is over soon for us all."

The ride to the main road leading to Warbow went silently. Now and then Arnold studied Larry. They came to the Rocking K line and Arnold pointed westward. "That's the way. Plan to come back here again?"

"Depends on your boss. I hope so."

Arnold reined around, leaving the road clear.

"There's Warbow. Take some advice, huh? . . . Stay there. If you come back because the boss invites you, keep your eyes and thoughts off her."

Arnold gave a hand flip of a farewell salute, set spurs, and rode at a defiant trot back toward home.

By the time Larry saw the first houses of Warbow he was only sure that Matt Arnold disliked him and that Carrie Keiler, attractive flirt, spelled trouble. As to Keiler himself, the little bantam could not bear the thought of another man who could perhaps counterorder him and still be obeyed. Recalling Captain Darnell, Larry wondered if this might not also be his key.

He came into town and rode toward the stable. As he dismounted, he heard a roll of hoofs and two grim-faced men rode by. The hostler appeared in the wide doorway and his head turned with Larry's to watch the men come to a near-sliding halt before the marshal's office and hurry within.

"Now what's got into them?" the hostler asked of the air as much as Larry.

"Know them?"

"Bart Flynn, the lean dark one. He owns Rafter F. The other one's his neighbor, the heavy blond man. Eric Hampton of Flying W. English combine owns it and Eric ramrods for 'em. Southwest of town, both spreads."

Larry gave the black gelding's reins to the hostler and walked to the marshal's office. He

56

heard an angry lift of voices that cut off short the moment his boot rapped on the wooden verandah floor.

Three men faced him when he stepped into the office. Banks stood behind his desk. The other two had obviously wheeled about, one lean and dark, with a trouble-scarred, youthful face and the other heavy and fair, with a thick shock of yellow hair and eyes a clear, pale blue, ice-hard at the moment.

Banks said, "Sorry, Crane. Law business."

"Who's he?" Flynn demanded.

"Lawrence Crane," Banks said. "Something of a big wheel with the railroad, sent out here to look us over."

"Not exactly," Larry protested. "I'm with the land—"

Flynn exclaimed, "I bought some of your range, part of my Rafter F. Good ranching country, you people told me. But you didn't say one damn word about rustlers!"

"Oh I say, Bart," Hampton objected. "Not his bloody problem, y'know."

Larry demurred, "Rustling country is trouble country for the railroad as well as you."

"Then do something about it!" Flynn snapped.

Larry threw a questioning glance at Banks, who shrugged. "Both Flynn and Hampton lost beef— last night, maybe yesterday. Fairly fresh sign, anyhow."

"And leading right to that damn camp!" Flynn added. "Nemeth put us onto them first and, sure enough, the sign headed right there before it wiped out."

"Who is Nemeth?"

"Small rancher down our way," Flynn answered Larry.

"Not exactly top-hole neighbor," Hampton added. "But he did see three or four soldiers near the range where our beef grazed. We picked up a trail that led toward the post."

Banks shook his head. "But it wiped out before it reached there, so you can't accuse—"

"Oh, not accuse!" Hampton corrected quickly. "But it would help no end if we knew that our beef's nowhere around the camp. Can't jibe at that, really?"

"Don't think Darnell won't!" Banks answered.

Flynn slammed a fist on the desk. "Who cares what Darnell thinks? That's my beef—and yours, Eric. What's stopping us from riding out there and looking around whether Darnell likes it or not?"

Larry answered in a level voice that cut through Flynn's anger. "Let's make a tally, friend. First, Marshal Banks' star is good to the town limits. He's not a sheriff because there's not even a county organized in this part of the territory. Second point, the camp out there, like any Army post, is under federal jurisdiction and not a sheriff's, even if you had one. So are the troops, each one, no matter where he is."

"Something like Queen's Law, what?"

"Something like, Mr. Hampton. That's why the marshal can't hold a trooper in jail and why Darnell won't let them be arrested."

"But, damn it!—"

Larry ignored Flynn's outburst. "Third, you have no proof of what this man Nemeth said or that any trooper touched your beef. Flynn, if you were faced with strangers on your own ranch who accused you of rustling and wanted to comb your herd, how would you act?"

Flynn grunted his surrender. "But we just can't let the thing go unchecked!"

Larry spoke to Banks. "Suppose the three of us ride out to C Troop? Three civilians curious to see a camp. I might even find railroad business to talk over with the captain. You could look around, ask a few questions. You might find out about your beef."

"Makes sense, y'know," Hampton said to Flynn.

"But where does Banks come in?" Flynn demanded.

"He doesn't," Larry pulled himself from the chair. "He has no right to be there officially. But the three of us . . ."

"Let's ride," Hampton decided.

"Give me time to get to the stable and back." Larry walked out the door.

He was several yards away when Banks came hurrying up. "You got me off a forked stick, Crane. But you need to know Darnell likes civilians just a little less'n he likes me. You could end up in his guard house. And say Flynn bellers too loud?"

Larry grinned. "Why, I'll have company in the guard house, Marshal."

Chapter VI

On the ride to C Troop's camp, Larry began to get to know his two companions. Bart Flynn rode with an intent singleness of purpose that was both praiseworthy and annoying. He was one of those men who would never ease down; it showed in the pull of cheeks and jaw toward a stubborn chin and a too rigid mouth.

Eric Hampton, on the other hand, rode with an easy confidence in himself. There was a faint reserve about him and even the laughter in his voice seemed to be held within bounds. But for all this, he had an easy friendliness, an air of letting come what may.

He could drop the problem and the errand at hand enough to be curious about Larry's job with the railroad and this irritated Flynn, who finally cut in on Hampton's questions to Larry. "Eric, we can tally one another later. The camp's just up ahead. We'd best figure what we're going to do."

"I say, don't we know that? We're riding in politely to look around. What we do depends on what we see. No use planning it until then, what?"

"But suppose we find the beef!"

"We'll go to the captain, old man. He can't just dismiss a crime, even if his own men are involved, you know. He can't very well pretend we're not there and do nothing about it, can he?"

Flynn frowned, rode on, tight-faced as Hampton unconcernedly continued his interrupted talk with Larry. "English and Scots money out here in Montana and Wyoming. Good investments, if there's someone here to muck about and keep an eye on things. Flying W, for instance, owned by a combine of two counts, a duke, and an earl. A royal ranch, by Jove! You people have fine agents in England, Crane. I daresay everywhere, eh?"

"I've heard that."

Hampton, riding more like a cavalry officer than a puncher, said, "I have word from a friend of mine in Scotland. Your agents reached him and some of his friends. They could be neighbors of ours up here. That is . . ."

Larry asked, "Something to prevent it?"

Flynn snapped, "Sure there is—Keiler! Scotland ain't Texas."

"But it's C&FW land we're selling," Larry protested.

"But Keiler runs the Warbow country, friend. He's made it plain he'll drive out all but Texans from now on. That is, after he drives out the U.S. Army."

"Speaking of the Army," Hampton said quietly, "we've met it."

Larry and Flynn swiveled heads in direction of his pointing finger. A single soldier sat his horse

62

on the crest of the swale. Golden late afternoon sunshine bathed him, casting half his face in deep shadow under the brim of his campaign hat. The soldier suddenly broke into motion, coming down the slope at an easy trot toward them.

"I say! It's Left'nant Eaton. That helps."

Lieutenant Eaton came up with a wide smile on his boyish face, gauntleted hand making a salute. "Mr. Hampton, sir! What brings you this way?"

"English curiosity about the American Army, for my part. Mr. Crane here would like to see Captain Darnell. You know Flynn, Left'nant? Of course! You met at my digs."

The officer looked to be a shade the right side of thirty, Larry judged, and perhaps six feet or more tall. The bone structure of the broad face was well formed and Larry looked at clear brown eyes that quickly, shrewdly, weighed and judged.

"Mr. Crane, sir. I'm First Lieutenant Eaton, executive officer for Captain Darnell. You're welcome to the camp, but may I ask your business with the captain?"

"A pleasure, Lieutenant. The railroad sent me to thank Captain Darnell and C Troop for the handling of the Indian trouble. I need to report back to Chicago the captain's judgment as to the chance of future outbreaks."

"There'll be no outbreaks, sir. But the captain will tell you that officially, if you'll ride with me." He swung around and the three men fell in with him. He asked Hampton, "And how is Miss Evelyn, sir?"

"Fine, Left'nant. We look to having you at Flying W again soon."

"Thank you. As soon as liberty permits."

They topped the rise and once again Larry looked down on the temporary post. Flynn's harried eyes swept over it for sign of beef, and he scowled when he saw none. The four men rode down the slope and a sentry stepped from a small building and saluted as Eaton rode by.

They crossed a rough parade ground and Eaton drew rein before a building that was little more than a shack. "Headquarters, gentlemen. I'll take you to the captain."

Hampton said easily, "Just Crane, Left'nant. Flynn and I will wander about, if it's permissible."

Eaton made them welcome with a wave of the hand. He pointed to one of three smaller shacks. "My quarters. My pleasure if all of you would drop in after Mr. Crane is through."

He led Larry to the low verandah of headquarters. A soldier at the door saluted and, within, a sergeant major came to standing attention behind a table serving as a desk. Eaton announced Crane.

A few minutes later, Larry stepped into a small office and Captain Darnell looked coldly at him, questioningly at Eaton. The lieutenant explained Larry's visit.

Only then did Darnell extend his hand and make a stiff polite wave to a chair before the table that also served him as a desk. Darnell looked shorter and stockier now that he did not wear the campaign hat; there was a hint of gray at the sideburns, and signs of petulance, pride, and frustration in the tanned, heavy features.

Darnell dismissed Eaton. Some of the rigidity left his voice and face. "A pleasure, Mr. Crane, to meet someone not connected with Warbow and cattle."

"In a way I am, sir."

"You're not a pinch-penny merchant, an unshaven cowboy or an insufferable rancher, sir. That's enough. I'm flattered the railroad comes to me about the Indian question. I'm sure C&FW has direct connections with the War Department in Washington."

"Washington is not Warbow, Captain. The Indians were here and might be again."

"No to both your statements, sir. I wish this were Washington—or almost any other place. There will be no further Indian trouble. Excuse my pride, but C Troop scared them out of their red hides and they won't be back."

"That's a relief! I can report to the Chicago office that we can go ahead with our plans. I'll quote you by name, if I may."

Darnell's tight lips actually softened. "Good of you, Mr. Crane. But no need."

65

"With the Indian trouble over, I suppose you'll be moving out of Warbow soon."

"Hard to say. We're waiting orders. No need to stay on, of course, but sometimes there are little delays."

"Just as with the railroad. By the way, Captain, I thought you handled the situation in town yesterday very quickly and very well."

"That's where I met you! I remember now." Darnell's face suffused with anger. "There's a bad element in Warbow, sir. They feel my troopers—the very ones who came to protect them—are less than dirt and can be cheated or trampled on at will. I protect my men."

"Bad element, Captain?"

"Texans! They think they stand big and proud and rule everything in sight. Of course, they hate a blue uniform and still try to fight a war that they lost years ago."

"Texans . . . yes. I've heard of a Keiler who owns the Rocking K."

"He is the worst of the lot, Mr. Crane." Darnell smacked palm on the table and his West Point ring made a harsh noise. "That man has the temerity to believe he rules the Army as well as those half-savage punchers and neighbors of his. Do you know, sir, he has given me orders to keep my men in camp, off the range, and out of town! He has tried to commandeer my men, in town and on the range, to help him hunt down cattle thieves! He has ordered me to leave the Warbow area, move C Troop without proper orders from my superiors! He is an insufferable egotist and boor, Mr. Crane."

"I've met him."

"Then you know, sir! I am sorry you saw that business the other day."

"You mentioned theft of cattle—"

"And some of those fools blame us—C Troop! Would you believe it?"

"Rustling makes everyone jumpy, Captain. I've heard the trail of the stolen beef often ends near the post. Coincidence, of course, and only that. But I can understand how rumors start."

"I know how to shut the mouth of the man who speaks them in my presence, sir. I'll have no slur on my command."

"I believe it, Captain. You're that kind of officer. You should be a major before long, I'd guess."

Darnell's eyes lighted and then gloomed. "Thank you, Mr. Crane. But there are few men in the Army now and far too many officers in proportion. Something like the old saying about too many chiefs and not enough Indians. We stay overage in rank these days, unfortunately."

Larry stood up as Darnell arose to show the interview was over. "Captain, you may be mistaken. You've done such good work here with the Indians and I'll pass your name on to the

Chicago office. Perhaps C Troop will be transferred. It would be a shame if some little thing held up your command."

Darnell stiffened. "What would there be, sir?"

Larry smiled. "I really was just thinking aloud, Captain. A wild guess by one who doesn't have the military mind, like you. Thank you and good day, sir."

Darnell hesitated a second, eyes sharp and searching. Then he called his sergeant major. "Have an orderly attend to Mr. Crane's mount, Sergeant."

Flynn and Hampton waited outside as Larry emerged. Lieutenant Eaton appeared at the same moment from his quarters. He again suggested the men stay, but Larry pled business in town and the two ranchers also declined.

They rode beyond the boundary of the camp, topped the ridge, and descended the far slope. Larry broke the silence. "No luck finding stolen beef, I take it."

"I hardly expected it, y'know," Hampton answered. He glanced at Flynn. "I know what Nemeth said, Bart, and the trail did come this way. But after all, those are soldiers back there. And frankly, old man, I'm not sure of Nemeth."

Back in Warbow, Larry parted from the two men. Flynn hardly answered his good-bye, but Hampton thanked him, and invited him to the Flying W. Larry checked his horse in the stable.

Weary with the day's long ride, he went to the hotel. After supper, he came out on the big verandah and found Banks seated alone in the gathering twilight shadows. The marshal pulled an empty chair around beside his own and said, as Larry sat down, "Heard you rode for nothing."

"Just about."

"Thought as much. What about Keiler and Darnell?"

"Hard to say. I gave 'em both the message. I think they caught it, especially Keiler. He didn't invite me back, despite Miss Carrie's hint before we started talking. Said he'd think things over and see me in town."

"Then he caught the idea. By the way, mind a word of warning? Matt Arnold thinks Carrie Keiler belongs to him. She has other ideas, being proud and pretty and liking attention. But Matt Arnold's not a man to tangle with."

"I don't intend to."

"Just keep that in mind, friend. Carrie likes to use her eyes on men, and that smile and walk of hers is about as bad. But—what about Darnell?"

"He wants C Troop moved out as bad as anybody else. I dropped the idea trouble might keep it here. He's overdue for promotion—"

"You didn't hint about that!"

"No, but I mentioned it and said he'll be named in all my reports. I can't help what he believes."

Banks leaned forward to look down the empty,

purple-shadowed street. "Peaceful and maybe you'll keep it that way. I wish to hell we could get C Troop out of here."

"Who listens to little frogs croaking? Give it time until someone somewhere in the Army finds they've lost some cavalrymen. About the only way it'll work out. What about Hampton and Flynn?"

"Mad, both of them, though Flynn shows it more than that Englishman. Trail lost and the lead Nemeth gave them blew up in their faces. They're calling it quits this time."

"How about next time—and next time—and other ranchers?"

"I keep thinking that myself. It's another thing ready to blow. I'll ride out tomorrow where the trail wiped out. I just might pick it up again. Wouldn't gamble on it, though."

"Mind if I ride along?"

"This is rustling, not railroad."

"Marshal, how can I get Gagnle selling Warbow range again if cattle keep disappearing?"

"All right. See you in my office first thing come morning. If you have a Colt, wear it. I'll furnish the rifle, since you'll be a deputy."

Chapter VII

The next day, Larry and Banks found the place where the trail of the stolen cattle had vanished. Banks looked slowly around. "It's like they didn't give a damn who followed 'em to here. And then the rustlers split up, riding off like spokes in a wheel. Which one do you follow? Bet you whichever one, it'll wipe out within a mile. Let's see if I'm right."

He indicated one of the branching signs. They followed it north and east, avoiding C Troop's camp. As Banks had predicted, the trail came to a small brook and vanished. Larry and Banks followed the brook, upstream and down, but there was no sign that rider and steer had left it.

Banks finally signaled Larry back across the stream and said, "We can go back and pick another. It'll do the same."

Larry eased in his saddle, aware of the unaccustomed weight of the deputy star sagging his left shirt front. He looked south toward the camp. "Troopers seen near where the beef was stolen," he mused aloud, "but point is, I can't believe troopers are rustlers. By the way, where does C Troop get its beef ration?"

"In Warbow. Richards at the general store buys from the ranches and resells it to C Troop."

"So there's no point in stealing. That's why Darnell is so blazing mad that there's even the suspicion against his men."

"Well," Banks stretched tired muscles, "we don't git far just jawing. Want to try another of these trail spokes?"

They returned to where the trail broke up and chose another of the "spokes." This led them closer to the camp and then veered to the traveled road where signs were obliterated by the overlying marks of a well-traveled trail. Nor could Larry or Banks find where the rider and stolen steer had turned off.

They returned to town and Larry stabled his horse, gave his badge back to Banks, and then walked thoughtfully to the land office. Gagnle looked up when he entered, pudgy face alight with hope. "Have you found anything, Mr. Crane? Will you be able to set things right?"

"Found out a good deal, Harve," Larry answered as he walked to the map. He spoke as he studied it. "But setting things right is something else."

"Oh," Gagnle's voice deflated. "I saw you ride out and back with Ralph Banks."

"I was curious about the rustling at Flying W and Rafter F. C Troop's camp doesn't show on the map. Where is it?"

"It's there above the surveyed railroad land, Mr. Crane. C Troop is on government land not yet homesteaded or surveyed, so it wouldn't show."

"Rocking K, Flying W, and Rafter F?" Larry asked and Gagnle pointed to red-colored sections. "And this man Nemeth?"

"Down here, between Flying W and Rafter F. Not much of an outfit."

Larry studied the small red area and then the ranches, town, and C Troop camp in relation to one another. He followed the drawn line of the railroad's angle across the map, through the town. Gagnle covertly studied Larry and finally ventured, "Then you don't think things will straighten out?"

"Sure—but it may take time. Any new leads on land buyers?"

"All backing off when they find out what's happening in Warbow."

"Well, keep with it, Harve. They'll start coming again."

Larry strolled slowly to the railroad station. The small waiting room, with its cold potbellied stove, was empty, but Larry heard sounds behind the closed ticket window. He tapped on the door beside it and the stationmaster answered.

Larry showed his identification and then indicated the stock pens along the far spur line. "Do you have small shipments of beef during the year, other than roundup time?"

"I wish we did. Warbow could use the freight money."

"West of here?"

"Not a cattle car outside regular seasons comes through Warbow, Mr. Crane."

With a picture of the map in his mind, Larry asked about the towns to the east. "Just a spur line and some pens and a station. The town itself sits about a mile or more north of the line. Jayhawk was built before the railroad come through and there was no point spending extra money to curve the rails up to it."

"Cattle shipments?"

"Don't know what Jayhawk station does, Mr. Crane. You'll have to ask down there. Jayhawk's some ride—'bout sixty miles. Easiest way is to hop the eastbound out of here."

Larry thanked him and returned to the hotel. He spent the rest of the day on the verandah, watching the life of the town, his mind always on the map and the lost trail of the stolen cattle.

Larry wandered over to the general store. Richards proved to be a rotund man of medium height sporting a thick, gray moustache that gave firmness to face and nose. He seemed glad that Larry broke the routine of the store and readily answered questions.

"Sure, C Troop trades with me. In that way, I'll be sorry to see 'em go. But in another way—well, they can't leave too soon. They get drunk on leave and they stiff-leg around town with chips on their shoulders. But I reckon you've heard all about that."

At Larry's further question, he took him out back to a small stock pen where two steers somnolently stood, tails swatting flies. "That's Nemeth beef right now. I buy from all but Rocking K. Keiler wants none of his stock feeding Yankee soldiers and, besides, he don't need the pin money. C Troop will drive those two steers to camp maybe Friday and they do their own slaughtering. That's why I can't understand talk about soldier rustling."

Larry returned to his verandah chair, thought a while longer and came to a decision. He went to his room, wrote a brief first-report to Reeves and Marlowe, merely stating the situation as he had found it and promising later reports. Captain Hale Darnell, true to his promise, was mentioned at least twice.

The next day, Larry buckled on gunbelt, rented a rifle and saddle scabbard from Richards, bought shells for it and his Colt, and went to the stable. He rode north out of Warbow and headed directly for the spot where the rustler's trail had vanished. He followed the "spoke" that led to the creek.

He drew rein there and called up his mental picture of the survey map. He remembered the drawing of this very stream and recalled its course. Then, not bothering to find sign of trail again, he followed it eastward. Soon he realized that he must now be riding through Rocking K range well to the north of the ranch house.

The stream suddenly elbowed directly south and Larry rode out from the stream in the general direction of distant Jayhawk station. He moved eastward in a series of north-south zigzags. Ten miles out, he topped the ridge of a deep swale and instantly drew rein.

Down below, the grass was trampled and he saw the black, ugly ring of a dead fire. He searched along the swale and along the ridges. Satisfied, he moved down the slope to the fire.

Sign indicated that men and cattle had gathered here and they had camped at least one night. The Rocking K crew would be too close to home to bother to camp, Larry knew. His eyes sparked eagerly as he guessed he had come on the place where the "spokes" had converged again.

He cast away from the fire and found the bedding ground for the cattle. Ten head, he judged from the sign, so more than Hampton and Flynn's beef had been stolen. The trail led eastward. Larry loosened the Colt in its holster and made sure of a bullet in the rifle chamber and set himself to follow the trail as fast as he could.

Some ten miles beyond, the swales grew less deep and farther apart and he came onto a generally even slope of land. He saw small clusters of hills here and there. It was all empty of movement or building. The trail led straight toward the nearest complex of hills, and sign was fresh. He had made faster time than the herd.

He came to the hills and followed the trail into a narrow, winding defile between them. He watched both ridges, defile ahead, and the trail just below his horse's nose. His right hand remained close to the holstered Colt as he pressed on.

He took a turn in the defile and saw the trail leading on to a far turn. Hills pressed close, as though he rode momentarily in a canyon. He touched spurs lightly and the black's speed increased. He was almost at the far end when a slight movement on a ridge caught his attention.

He sawed back on the reins and the black half-wheeled. He saw no further movement up on the ridge and he began to wonder if his first impression had been right. He swung the black to the trail again and, up on the ridge, light made a bright glinting pinpoint for a second.

Someone was watching him through binoculars up there among the grass and bushes. Again Larry drew rein. A second later something made a wasp-crack through the air to his left and he heard the flat slam of a rifle up on the ridge.

Chapter VIII

Larry's hand dropped to his rifle and half jerked it from the scabbard. He realized the futility of it, bent low and set spurs. The horse wheeled about with a snort. Another bullet whipped close.

The horse raced back down the defile. A third slug whined high and uselessly to speed Larry on his way. He rounded the far turn, safe from the bullets for the moment. He drew rein, his mind racing.

He had pressed too closely on the rustlers and a rear guard had spotted him. That glint of binoculars told Larry the outlaw had a very close look and would know him. Larry made a faint grimace at the realization of the other's advantage. But now he considered the trail, the ridges above him. Down here in this pocket he would have no chance and an unseen rifleman could work around for another shot. Or he'd give the alarm and the whole bunch, whatever their number, would be after him.

Larry reluctantly rode back down the defile the way he had come. There would be another time and place, and already he knew very much more than the rustlers realized. He did not fully lose the crawling sensation along his back until he broke free of the hills and rode out well beyond rifle shot.

Back in the town, he rode directly to the station and sent a telegram to the stations along the line, east and west. He asked if any of them had received small shipments of beef. If so, would they report to him. Then Larry rode to the stable. Rifle returned to Richards, he started across the street to the hotel but turned when Banks hailed him.

"Thought I'd tell you. Maybe twenty soldiers are in town on liberty and acting peaceful as parsons. Figure it's a sign your talk with Darnell did some good?"

"Might be. When Rocking K and C Troop meet, we'll have our answer."

"Reckon so. Been riding out?"

"Thought about those rustlers and—"

"Shucks! Give it up. I've worn a law badge too many years in too many places to try to find a cold and gone trail. Like I said, let's hope for luck next time."

Larry started to protest but then grinned as he thought of the surprise he might give the lawman. He waved and turned back across the street to the hotel. Good man, Banks, he thought, but a shade too confident. To shake that confidence a bit might do him good.

The next day, Larry checked the station and found replies to his telegrams. No one reported small shipments but Jayhawk, the last one there over a month ago. Larry thought of the trail he had followed. Over a month ago, he thought as he walked to the stable, but none just yesterday or today.

He rode out of Warbow, heading south and west. He set a steady pace and the long miles dropped behind him. Some distance on, the main road ended and a narrower road curved from it, the sign indicating Flying W—Bristol Associates. Larry turned toward the distant ranch.

He had ridden about a mile or so when he saw a bunch of cattle far off to his right. A moment later, he saw a rider cut away from the bunch and come at a fast trot toward him. Larry reined in to wait.

As the rider neared, he recognized Eric Hampton. At the same moment, Hampton lifted his horse to a gallop and swiftly came up, reined in, and smiled warmly. "Mr. Crane! Good to see you again, sir. I say, I didn't expect the honor so soon."

"I wanted to talk to you and remembered your invitation so—"

"Here you are! The house is along the road a bit. Shall we? A new face at Flying W is welcome—perhaps more than welcome because it's new, y'know."

Larry smiled his thanks. Hampton talked as they rode, of the weather and beef prices, speaking of the Flying W and its work with a quiet pride that Larry liked. They came on another of those small valleys that seemed characteristic of the country. A creek snaked its way through the valley; Flying W ranch buildings were strung along its banks: main house, bunkhouse, cook shack, and barn in a line, the corrals and pens forming a small tangle of neatly painted white. Larry noticed a splash of color beside the house bordered with dark green hedge.

Hampton caught his faint surprise. "Bit of English garden transported here, as much as Montana can nourish English plants, y'know. My wife and Evelyn tend it."

"You must feel lonely."

"Not really—nostalgia, mostly. We're much too busy to be lonely."

They had approached the house now. It looked sturdy and well-kept and the grass about it was neatly cropped, The road at this point had been lined with stones, each whitewashed and faultlessly clean.

The main entrance was a wide, thick door, flanked by windows, set deep under overhanging eaves. It opened as Larry and Hampton rode up and a woman stood framed. The men dismounted and Hampton led Larry up to the door. Larry swept off his hat and Hampton said, "Mr. Lawrence Crane, m'dear. The railroad man I told you about. This is my wife."

Mrs. Hampton had a slender, stately pride as natural as her smile of welcome and her extended hand. She had light brown eyes and hair, but her skin was fair and smooth. Slightly clipped but

81

friendly words made Larry welcome and she led the way inside.

Neither house nor room had the pretentiousness of Rocking K. Larry liked the unobtrusive furniture, which must have been brought from England. Mrs. Hampton asked polite questions about Larry's work.

At last she stood up. "You'll want to talk business with Eric, I'm sure. Then he'll want to show you Flying W. We're very proud of it, y'know. My daughter is out riding somewhere, but she'll be back and we'll show you the garden. By then, it will be time for dinner."

"That would be an imposition!"

"Mr. Crane, it is a Flying W habit to hold visitors just as long as we possibly can." She continued imperturbably, "By the time dinner is over, it will be much too late to return to Warbow —y'see, I've blocked an objection—and we have a comfortable guest room."

She smiled and walked away before Larry could say a word. Hampton chuckled. "No use fighting, old man. Besides, you'd find all of us against you. How about a spot of whiskey?"

Soon they were seated comfortably in big chairs near one of the windows. Larry asked how the railroad could improve cattle shipping. Hampton said he was satisfied. Railside pens were adequate and, so far, strings of cars had been spotted without delay.

Larry directed the talk to rustled cattle. Hampton admitted there had been a steady trickle of theft throughout the whole Warbow area. Remembering the Jayhawk telegram, Larry asked if there had been a theft a month or so before.

"Half a dozen Rocking K beef, as I remember. Keiler had the whole crew scouring the country. Matt Arnold, by the way, would be the man to shoot a rustler on sight. Handsome man, Arnold, but I'd say something of a brute."

"They found nothing?"

"Nearly a war with the United States Army. Keiler and Arnold demanded the right to search the camp. I hear Captain Darnell nearly had them shot out of hand. Those two will start a bloody war yet."

"How many time have the rustlers hit you?"

"Once that I'm sure of. Winter before last we lost a few head, but they could have just drifted off ahead of snow and wind."

"Nemeth saw drifting soldiers near where your beef was stolen. How about the other times?"

Hampton refilled Larry's glass. "I don't know that Nemeth started the earlier talk. It just started going around, y'know."

"What about Nemeth? Trust him?"

"No reason why I shouldn't—but I don't really. He came up with the first trail herd Keiler drove from Texas, then quit or was discharged. I've heard it both ways. He filed on a section of homestead land. So, he's my neighbor and Flynn's. Doesn't bother us."

"Crew?"

"Oh, maybe three or four, sometimes just Nemeth himself. Again, I've heard there'll be a dozen men at Box N. Seen some of 'em and I wouldn't want 'em working here."

Larry heard a faint drum of hoofs, but they faded and Hampton continued talking about his neighbor with a faint note of distaste. After some moments, the door swung back and a girl burst into the room and came to a surprised, abrupt halt when she saw Larry.

She was as tall as Hampton and had his wife's slenderness. Her hair was brown, her longish face smoothly tanned, and her eyes blue. Slender of figure, she wore a formal riding habit that could not conceal the curve of her breasts and hips, and that accented her long, shapely legs.

Hampton said, "Evelyn, this is Mr. Crane, from the railroad. My daughter, Mr. Crane."

She came forward with a boyish, graceful stride, extending her hand. "I imagine Mums has insisted on dinner with us."

"And a tour of the garden," he added.

"Then I'll change to something more appropriate if you'll excuse me, Mr. Crane."

After she had left, Larry said, "A lovely daughter, sir."

"Thank you. I notice all young men are aware of Evelyn."

"It can't be helped." Larry remembered. "Lieutenant Eaton asked about her the other day."

"One of the 'aware' young men, including you."

Despite his earlier determination, Larry could not readily ride away from Flying W. Mrs. Hampton appeared and then Evelyn came down, dressed in light summery colors, her hair done in a high swirl that disclosed a full forehead and small, delicate ears. It heightened her cheekbones, lengthened and thinned her face.

The women took Larry out to the flower garden and he admired the blooms as they slowly paced the spacious area within the low, thick hedge. They returned to the house and Mrs. Hampton excused herself.

"I must see how the cook does."

She left them alone. Evelyn indicated a nearby chair. "Father said you are a railroad man, Mr. Crane. Something like an engineer or Mr. Gagnle in Warbow?"

"Something like Mr. Gagnle, only more so." That led to her question about the railroad land. Her interest led him on and he became very much aware of her slightly parted lips, the deep concentration of blue eyes that silently applauded and admired both the railroad's work and his own.

"But now," he finished, "this is unfair. What about you?"

She sketched her life with a faintly mocking humor as she spoke of the England she knew, of the girls' school she had attended that tried to be exclusive. She spoke of travel in France, Germany, and Italy with her parents.

"Then Father decided to come on to America and here I am," she finished.

Larry could not help comparing her with Harriet Reeves. They were so completely different in heritage, background, and education, and yet they were similar. It puzzled him, but suddenly he had it. Life had given both women poise and something intangible that Larry could only call culture. Transfer either girl to the other's life and she would be almost at home.

Mrs. Hampton and her husband interrupted the conversation. Hampton escorted Larry to a spacious room and left him with word to "come down" in half an hour. Larry looked around the comfortable, airy room with pleasure. As he washed his face, rearranged his string tie, and combed his hair, he thought of Evelyn. She was a woman any man would be proud to know. Like Harriet, he thought abruptly, with a wry smile. And just as fleetingly met. No wonder Lieutenant Eaton showed interest. Larry, with faint regret at his own situation, wished the young officer luck.

Back in the main room, Larry discovered the lamps lit and dark drapes drawn. He might have been in a Chicago or New York drawing room rather than in the wide, barren sweep of Montana. Hampton served whiskey for the men and sherry for the women. Mrs. Hampton proved as graciously curious as Evelyn.

Dinner was excellent and Larry mentally bet the cook in the kitchen was Montana-taught and English-finished, probably by Mrs. Hampton. Steaks and vegetables were strictly Western American, but the trimmings were strange, delicious, and English.

Back in the main room, Hampton showed joyful surprise to know Larry played whist and the four of them sat down to a couple of hours of it. They tired of it, finally, and Evelyn showed her disappointment as her parents pointed out the late hour. She gave Larry an underbrow look and suggested a walk.

Mrs. Hampton said in disapproval, "I'm sure Mr. Crane must be tired, my dear."

Evelyn, with a faint pout, surrendered to her mother's English sense of propriety. She made her "Good night," her hand resting a bit long in Larry's, then left with her mother.

Hampton stifled a yawn. "A nightcap's in order, isn't it?"

As Hampton poured, Larry's eyes strayed to the hallway down which the women had disappeared. He felt a lift of excitement. Evelyn Hampton intrigued him.

Chapter IX

Back in Warbow early the next afternoon, Larry wrote a report to Jepson detailing his conversations with Keiler and Darnell, and he told of his veiled hints to both men as to the railroad's possible pleasure or displeasure.

"C&FW is not officially committed to what I said," he wrote frankly, "but both of these men need a checkrein. I wish that C Troop could get moving orders. That would leave but two problems—Keiler's attempt to rule the roost and the rustling."

He posted the letter with a hope that Jepson, or Marlowe in Chicago, would not reprimand his use of the railroad as a threat; but there was a counter consideration. He had been sent to clear up Warbow's trouble as far as the railroad was involved and he had the hunch that Jepson would not mind boldness.

The town was quiet and Larry returned to the hotel and sat on the shaded verandah. He fell in with the somnolent mood of the town. His drifting thoughts slowly came to a focus on Warbow. If he could resolve the problem here, he would have played an important part in birthing the huge ranches that were bound to come.

His thoughts extended into the future as he

envisioned the network of rails already beginning to reach westward across the country. Larry might be given a part to play at any spot from timbered Oregon or fishing Puget Sound to Texas or anywhere in between. The scope of his job and his opportunity sent a rush of pride and confidence coursing through him. He'd help build an empire!

Then he chuckled. It just might happen, if . . . There it was—Warbow. Here was his first assignment of importance and here he'd prove himself or fail. The future depended upon what happened in that sleepy, empty street or on the range round about.

Suddenly Evelyn Hampton's picture came clear in his mind with a faint excitement. Something of a world traveler, with innate culture and poise, as well as pretty and warm, Evelyn could not easily be dismissed from any man's mind. Why from his?

He mentally answered with a laugh at himself. "No reason, Crane, except you're building a lot on nothing. You met her once. She's friendly. She wanted to walk in a garden. She held your hand a second longer than you expected. Forget it."

He proceeded to try by spending the remainder of the afternoon with Gagnle in the land office. He reviewed queries and prospects with the agent and at last he indicated the papers with a wide wave of his hand.

"Every one of them is good, Harve."

"But, Mr. Crane! These are no good until you've done something."

Larry had walked to the map and he whipped around, half angry that Gagnle so readily threw full responsibility at him. The man sat at one end of the desk, shoulders rounded, pudgy hands splayed out on the papers and round face heavy with discouragement. Larry sighed.

"Such as answering those queries, Harve? Telling the nervous ones it's not as bad as it sounds and they should come to Warbow and see for themselves?"

Gagnle made an apologetic gesture. "No, Mr. Crane, I can do that."

Larry took a deep breath. "Please do. It'll leave me with the routine stuff to handle."

He strode out of the office, leaving Gagnle watching him with a stricken look.

The soldiers came into town that night, under the leadership of Lieutenant Eaton. The young officer rode ahead of the wagons carrying the troopers, leading them to the vacant area in front of the station. Eaton talked to them for a few moments, then the men streamed toward the nearest saloons.

When Larry turned into the dining room, Eaton hailed him from a nearby table. Larry joined him. They gave their order to the waitress and then Larry asked, "On liberty or duty?"

"The captain sent me in to see that C Troop behaves itself while it has fun. We've been blamed for everything from rustling to rowdy drunk, so the captain wants an officer around. I'm to make sure that if anything happens, it won't be our men who start it."

Their food came and Larry ate in silence. Had Darnell acted on the hint Larry had dropped? Now if only Keiler would make a like move!

Larry finished the meal and had coffee with Eaton, both men sitting at ease. Eaton seemed more handsome than Larry had first thought. His eyes sharpened critically as he studied his companion. Tall, blond, an officer. A woman could very easily become attracted, Larry thought. As though Eaton had caught his thought, he said, "Been to Flying W yet?"

Larry hid his start. "Yes, once."

Eaton asked almost too casually, "You met the family?"

"Both Mrs. and Miss Hampton are gracious hostesses."

"I go there often," Eaton commented. Larry let his silence answer.

Eaton toyed with his empty coffee cup, not knowing exactly how to break the impasse of Larry's silence. At last he clinked cup into saucer. "I'd better make a patrol and see that everything's all right."

"Can I stand you a drink later?"

"You can. Say the Rancher's Brand."

Eaton gave him a half salute and strode out of the room. Larry sat a while longer, then strolled out on the verandah. Full night had come and Warbow crouched under a panoply of bright stars in soft black sky. Lamplight barred the street here and there, streaming through doors and windows. Here on the porch, diffused light gave half-substance to chairs, porch rail, and ornate posts. At the far end, two drummers sat in close talk, cigars glowing and fading erratically like fireflies.

Larry dropped into a chair, after pulling it closer to the rail. He hooked boots on the rail so that his long legs made an inclined, ascending plane. He half watched the street as his thoughts moved to Eaton, Evelyn, and himself. He wondered why he had felt a stir of rivalry. He recalled his comparison of her with Harriet Reeves and then he wondered why he set Harriet up as a standard. Well . . . beautiful, self-assured, aware of her femininity and proud of it. A woman a man could not ever forget and could want but . . . Ah, Larry thought, there's why she's the standard. The unobtainable! Jepson Reeves' niece, so not ever for a land agent recently promoted supervisor. She moved in a wealthy social circle that knew New York, Boston, Washington, and burgeoning San Francisco. Vice-presidents for Harriet Reeves, no less. But

Evelyn Hampton, rancher's daughter? Sooner or later a man found a woman attuned to him and—

"Crane, you can sure hide yourself in dark corners!"

Larry's booted feet dropped to the floor with a crash. Marshal Ralph Banks loomed over him, grinning. "You act like you shot up the town and I caught up with you."

Larry laughed. "Caught up with me you did." He sobered. "Something wrong?"

Banks pulled up a chair. "Just the opposite! A third of C Troop is drinking, gambling, chucking the right girls under the chin, hitting all the bars—and Warbow's quiet!"

"Sure, I know, but the proof—"

"Rocking K, you said. Well, Matt Arnold's in with half a dozen riders spoiling to prove they're Texans and can take a dozen troopers each and win. But C Troop acts like Darnell gave 'em religion. They're peaceful lambs."

"Lieutenant Eaton came along to keep an eye on 'em."

"I wish Arnold would keep a check on Rocking K. But he'd be the first to find himself a fight." Banks stood up. "I'd best git along and keep the lid on, if I can."

"Heading toward the Brand? I'll go with you."

As they walked down the street, Larry immediately became aware of the activity. From the

Oxbow and the two gambling halls, punchers moved out onto the street only to enter the place next door or the one across the street. Larry saw no sign of the troopers.

The Brand catered to the ranch owners and foremen and had very little of the typical punchers' saloons along the street. The lamps were held in brackets of an ornate brass chandelier. The floor was smooth, polished, and swept, clear of sawdust. There were fewer tables, and the chairs were not the serviceable but hard straightbacks. The walls were papered and the mirror behind the bar had an expensive crystal-like quality to it.

Banks and Larry came to the bar. Except for the men at a table and two at the bar, the place was empty. Larry instantly recognized Matt Arnold at the bar. The Rocking K foreman glanced in the mirror, saw Larry's reflection, and his face hardened. But he also saw Banks and returned to his half-whispered talk with his companion.

Larry bought a drink for Banks. When the bartender had left, Banks said in a low voice, "You asked about Nemeth. That's him with Arnold."

At first glance, Nemeth seemed to be short. Then Larry realized the man hunched over his drink and that his stocky powerful body added to the illusion. His features were heavy, his nose gross and naturally flattened, the nostrils wide.

His eyes were deep-set in bunches of flesh below and heavy bone of brows above. His head was round, and there seemed to be no neck at all.

Banks added, "Keiler's not in town or those two wouldn't be talking. Nemeth and Arnold drove Texas trail herd for several years."

"First good thing I've heard about Arnold. He keeps a friendship despite his boss."

"Happens to trail partners sometimes."

Arnold suddenly swung around and, in the mirror, Larry saw that Eaton had entered. The officer stood a moment just within the batwings and Arnold hooked his elbows on the bar. Nemeth jabbed Arnold with his elbow. "Leave it lay, Matt."

"Ed wouldn't like that."

"To hell with Ed! You'n me—"

Nemeth broke off, searching toward Banks and Larry. Now Eaton had seen Larry and he came at an easy walk toward the bar. Nemeth left the bar, working his way along the far wall toward the batwings. Eaton came up, nodded to Banks, and said to Larry, "Sorry to be late. I'll have that drink now."

"Keeping your toy soldiers in line?"

Eaton swung around. His pleasant smile vanished and Larry looked on the face of the fighting soldier. Eaton's eyes veiled and he turned his back on Arnold, throwing over his shoulder, "They're in line."

Larry bought the round of drinks. The moment the bartender had left, Arnold asked, "Tell me, do they leak sawdust if you punch 'em hard enough?"

Eaton stiffened. Banks dropped his hand on the blue sleeve and turned to Arnold. "Tell you what I might do, Matt, if trouble breaks. I'll bend a gun barrel over a foreman's head and throw him in a cell just waiting for him."

Matt's eyes grew mean. "Reckon you can keep the jigger in there?"

"It's a good tight cell. The jigger'd be safe in there unless some of his foolish friends tried to break him out. That'd make bullets fly. Trouble in a thing like that, can't tell who a bullet'd hit, can you?"

"You wouldn't dare, Banks."

"Of course I wouldn't. It'd be a plumb bad accident. Like one of his own friends just fired blind." Banks gave a mock sigh. "Never had anything like that happen in my jail before. Pity!" Then he laughed. "Of course, we're talking just supposin', ain't we?"

Eyes held; then Arnold spat at the base of the bar and started to turn. Banks' easy voice checked him. "No matter who starts the trouble, I always go after the he-coon."

Matt Arnold stalked out of the saloon. Banks turned to the bar. "Matt will stand hitched—I think. But Keiler's going to hear a botched-up story about it. Seems like there's no way I can get along with Rocking K!"

Half an hour later, Larry left Banks and Eaton and started back toward the hotel. He saw some troopers leave a saloon and pass a knot of cowboys at the hitch-rack. The punchers moved to face the troopers; their very silence seemed blasphemous. The soldiers bunched, moved slowly in a wide arc out into the street, and then continued on their way. The cowboys turned as the troopers circled about them. One of them gave a loud guffaw, said something, and the bunch moved into the saloon.

Larry moved on. He felt restless and the hotel and its bare room did not appeal to him. He walked north to the edge of the town and stood alone in the dark, feeling the closeness of earth, sky, and stars. Then, reluctantly, he turned back along the dark street.

He passed the general store and saddlery shop, then came abreast of the barbershop next to the livery stable. He heard muffled, angry voices, but could see no one in the street. Then he realized they came from the dark area between the barbershop and stable.

". . . he's on to part of it, anyhow."

A growl answered, "Then take care of it."

"There ain't been any killing yet and there won't be. I don't want a hangnoose around my neck and that's exactly what it'd be."

Larry stood frozen before the recessed entry of the barbershop. The two men, whoever they were, stood within the areaway, off the street. Larry wondered that they hadn't heard his steps.

"No guts," the accusing growl came.

"Not when the trail would lead directly to me —and you can bet on it!"

"All right, I'll figure something out. But we ain't going to let the whole thing go belly-up because of him. Git home and stay low. If things begin to happen, just hang and rattle until I get out your way."

"Now wait a minute! What do you plan to do?"

"Throw a bone between the hungry dogs and let 'em fight. While that's going on, we take care of this jigger and everybody blames the dogs. Now git along."

Larry whipped into the deep recess. Steps became loud and then began to fade. He peered cautiously down the street. Lined against the distant light from saloons, he saw a powerful, stocky figure, head bent forward.

Larry ducked back within the recess. He waited. Five minutes passed and no near sound broke the silence. Then Larry realized the passageway between shop and stable was probably open on both ends. The second man had simply walked away in that direction.

Larry stepped out and peered down the dark area. Nothing moved, the passage devoid of life.

Larry turned and walked slowly to the hotel. That stocky figure had a puzzling familiarity. But the other, the second man, was no more than a growling voice.

Even though he didn't understand the conversation, Larry felt a cold chill for the man who had caught "on to part of it."

And who were the hungry dogs?

Chapter X

The morning was bright with sun and a breeze stirred the window curtains as Larry shaved. He had a feeling that this was the kind of day when he'd be lucky. Lucky—like C Troop moving out or Ed Keiler coming in to say he'd be a good boy, or Banks catching the rustlers. His bright mood lasted through breakfast and he whistled as he strolled down the street to the station. He heard the chatter of the telegraph and when he went inside and peered through the bars of the ticket window, the stationmaster looked up from the erratically clicking key.

"You come at the right time, Mr. Crane," he said, still transcribing the chatter to a flimsy. "This is for you—from Jayhawk station."

Larry waited impatiently until the key fell silent; the man ripped the page off the pad and brought it to the window.

"Twenty head cattle shipped yesterday. Mixed brands. Shipper Guy Lamping. KC buyer."

It was signed by Walling, stationmaster at Jayhawk. Larry folded the paper and put it in his pocket. "When's the next eastbound?"

"With luck, around noon. Without luck, from an hour to a week later. Catching it?"

"Yep, and I have the luck. It'll be on time."

Not quite, as Larry discovered. It was two hours late. He had it flagged for a stop, swung aboard, and was on his way to Jayhawk. It was nearly dusk when the train began to slow and the conductor said, "Your stop, Mr. Crane."

He swung off the coach steps as the train moved slowly into the station. The conductor instantly signaled and the train picked up speed. Looking about, Larry realized why he had not noticed the station on his journey to Warbow. The building sat alone in a vast wheel of land and darkening sky. He saw a dirt road leading northward to the town itself. A lamp glowed in one station window.

A man came out, stared. "I thought Number Eight slowed down! Mostly it don't even do that."

"You're Walling?"

"That's right."

"I'm Lawrence Crane. You sent me a wire about cattle shipments."

The man indicated the pens across the tracks. "Empty now, Mr. Crane."

"I'm interested in past shipments out of Jayhawk—when and who made 'em."

A short time later, Larry had a picture of the usual heavy roundup shipments as well as the steady trickle throughout the year. The manifests gave the shipper as Guy Lamping. Walling said, "Lamping's still in town, Mr. Crane. I drive back and forth in a buggy. I'll take you. Bring you back to catch whatever train you want."

It was almost dusk when the buggy rolled into Jayhawk itself. The town proved to be smaller than Warbow, with but two saloons, a single general store, and a hotel that Larry eyed with a dubiousness that Walling caught.

"Beds ain't much, I hear, but the cooking's good. Lamping's staying there."

Larry cast his eye down the short block of business structures, mostly one and two storys with false fronts. "No sheriff?"

"No law. We figure to organize Jayhawk County in a year or two. Have one then."

Larry climbed out of the buggy and Walling handed down his carpetbag. "I'll drop by the hotel come morning."

Larry thanked him and walked into the hotel. The lobby was very small. The room held ancient odors from cabbage boiled long ago and many times, an equally ancient bacon smell and, underlying all, undisturbed dust.

Larry's fist on a flat bell eventually brought a man in shirt sleeves. He wore no collar and looked as tired and old as the hotel. Larry signed the register, accepted the big key, and asked, "How about meals?"

"Supper at five, but I reckon Maw could scare up something for you. We ain't too busy at meal time. Just me'n her and a cattle buyer. Now you."

"Buyer this time of year?"

"Guy's in and out most every month. You'll meet him come breakfast if not before."

Though it had been "scared up," Larry had no fault to find with his lonely meal. Later, he wandered out on the porch. It was empty and he stood uncertain. He would like to meet Lamping by apparent accident and that precluded asking his room number and going up.

The light of the single saloon attracted him and he wandered over. Like the rest of Jayhawk, it looked depressed and deserted except for the bartender and a man playing solitaire at one of the tables.

Larry ordered a drink and commented, "Not much doing."

The bartender shrugged. "Not Saturday and it ain't regular shipping time. The place gets crowded then. You a new drummer?"

"No, railroad agent, in a way."

The man at the table looked up. "Walling going to leave or something?"

Larry turned. "Not at all. I drift around looking things over."

"Sort of a boss, huh?"

"In a way."

"Come sit down, friend. You get stuck in Jayhawk times like these and you like to share a drink. That is, if you're willing?"

"I'm willing—if you'll share a second with me."

"Now there speaks a gentleman! Pat, bring a bottle and glass for Mister . . . Mister . . . ?"

"Crane, Larry Crane."

"I'm Guy Lamping."

Lamping wore an ugly brown suit with black, thin stripes. His brown bowler hat sat on the edge of the table. He was not tall and his shoulders looked slightly rounded. His face was sallow, broad at the cheekbones. Though brown eyes had lighted with pleasure, Larry noted the way in which they constantly shifted, resting squarely one second and avoiding directness the next.

He had long, crooked and mobile lips, liver colored. He smiled constantly and his lips had a strange reptile way of moving back over his teeth. Larry found himself repelled by the lips but charmed by the wide, warm smile they finally formed.

Larry sat down and Pat brought the bottle and glass. Lamping swept the cards aside and poured for them both. "To your health, sir, and the continued health of the railroad. I depend on it."

"Oh?"

"Beef shipments, Crane. I'm a buyer. Oh, not a big one like those that come from Chicago. Ten head now, twenty this month, five-ten-twenty next month. Here in Jayhawk and wherever else I can make a deal."

"We're glad for the business. You surprise me.

I'd not think there'd be enough beef during the year to bring a buyer."

Lamping laughed, a strange choke in the throat and snort through the nose. "That's where you're mistaken. You'd be surprised how many ranchers like to pick up a few dollars, especially when the money sock grows empty between roundups. Always someone with a head or two to sell if you find 'em."

"But not at high prices."

"Sure not. A man selling offseason either needs the money or needs to get rid of the cows in a hurry. So long as he gives me bill of sale, I don't ask questions. I make a living, Crane, buying low and selling high as I can."

"Do you buy up around Warbow?"

"Don't have to. There's a drover up that way sort of covers it for me."

"When I get to Warbow, I'll look him up."

Lamping's eyes grew cautious and then he laughed again. "No you don't! I want him driving here and shipping through *me*. Think I'm going to let you cut out my profit?"

Lamping poured another drink and changed the subject by asking about the extent of the C&FW. "I talk beef and prices, dicker and dicker day in and day out. Come a time like tonight, the business all done, I want to forget it. Tell me about the railroad."

After several more attempts, Larry realized he

was beaten for the time being, and he dared not press too far. But by the time he left Lamping, still at the table with the whiskey bottle and the scattered playing cards, Larry knew that he had almost made the connection between the Warbow rustling and the Jayhawk beef shipments.

The next morning, in the dining room, Larry saw Lamping at a far table. His sallow face looked even more yellow. He stared morosely at Larry and murmured a grudging greeting. Larry, sensing the rebuff, took another table.

Sometime after, Larry stopped on his way out. "I ain't really unfriendly, Crane. There was just too much whiskey left in that bottle last night. Hope to meet you again sometime."

"Leaving town?"

"Buying again, way north and east of here. I figure to give your railroad more business soon if I'm lucky. I always ship from here."

"Then I might see you again."

Lamping nodded and walked out of the room. Not long afterward, Walling came into the lobby, saw Larry and came to the table. Larry motioned him to sit down and offered coffee. "I talked with Lamping. He says he buys from a drover from over Warbow way. Happen to know who it would be?"

Walling shook his head. Larry protested, "But you and Lamping don't put the beef in the cars yourself!"

"Just punchers, as far as I know, Mr. Crane. Of course, one of 'em could be the drover."

Larry rubbed his jaw, mind gnawing at the problem. "Is Lamping the only one who ships offseason? . . . Good, then make him show his bill of sales. Note the signers and the brands. Send the names and brands to me at Warbow. Now, when does the westbound go through?"

"Maybe two hours. I come to see if you wanted to go to the station."

Back at Warbow a little after noon, Larry first alerted the stationmaster to probable telegrams from Jayhawk. "Get them to me right away, at the land office or hotel. And keep your mouth shut about all this business. That's a warning."

The man stared, gulped, and nodded.

As Larry walked to the hotel, he saw some blue uniforms and wondered if Lieutenant Eaton still chaperoned his tough fighting men. He saw a buggy at the general store hitch-rack and noticed the Flying W brand on the horse's flank.

In his hotel room, Larry freshened up as he reviewed the time in Jayhawk and decided he had done as well as he could. He could only wait for developments. The thought of patient waiting until some unknown made a meaningful move made Larry restless. He shrugged into his coat and fled the four walls.

He descended the stairs with a clatter and almost plunged into the lobby. He pulled up short, as Lieutenant Eaton turned to face him. The young officer stood beside Evelyn Hampton who had turned about, puzzled by the noise Larry had made. Her face lighted. "Why, Mr. Crane! Father heard you were out of town."

"I just returned."

"I—Father will be delighted to see you again. Oh, have you met Lieutenant Eaton?"

"We've had the pleasure," Eaton said a bit stiffly.

"It would be so nice if you could both come to Flying W soon."

"My liberties might not always suit Mr. Crane's free time."

"Oh, dear!" Then she smiled directly at Larry, giving Eaton a portion of it. "Well, *either* of you are welcome."

The three of them stood in a strained silence which Eaton broke with an ease Larry admired: "Miss Evelyn, shall we see if your father has finished at the store?"

She gave Larry an underlash look that begged forgiveness. "I suppose we should." She brightened. "Perhaps Mr. Crane . . . ?"

Larry caught Eaton's heightening color. "I'd like to, but Mr. Hampton will be busy and so am I, unfortunately. But do give him my regards."

He smiled and left the hotel. He regretted walking off from Evelyn, but he had been too much aware of Eaton's growing stiffness. He turned in at the land office. Gagnle had gone out somewhere and Larry felt relief. He looked out the window and watched Evelyn Hampton and Eaton cross the street to the store. Larry watched her graceful walk and realized more forcefully than ever her eye-holding figure.

The two disappeared within the store, but Larry stood unmoving at the window. At the first opportunity he'd return to Flying W. Remembering Evelyn's eyes a few moments ago, he determined to avoid the whist. A stroll with Evelyn in the soft night would be worth the manipulations it would entail.

A figure darkened the door and Larry wheeled about, expecting Gagnle. The stationmaster said in relief, "Mr. Crane, glad I found you. This just come from Jayhawk."

He took the flimsy and read, "Lamping back late afternoon. Wants three cattle cars spotted siding four days from now. Won't say where beef to come from. Thought you should know. Walling."

Larry studied the flimsy, his mind racing. Lamping had ridden out of Jayhawk and returned as soon as Larry had left! Had the buyer been suspicious? Four days from now . . . and thirty to forty head. From where?

Larry looked up at the hovering stationmaster. "Send Walling a wire. Tell him I'll be there in four days."

The man, bursting with curiosity, left the office reluctantly. A second later, Larry saw Hampton and Evelyn ride by in the buggy, obviously headed back to Flying W. Larry felt a surge of disappointment.

Then the thin paper in his fingers drew his attention.

Chapter XI

Larry debated most of the evening as to whether he should tell Marshal Banks about the telegram. He met Banks at the Brand that night and had a strong impulse to tell him. But what? A shady buyer sixty miles away planned to ship beef. What does that have to do with Warbow? Larry could almost hear Banks' voice. Well, Larry mentally answered, it just might tie in with a rustling trail I followed east thirty miles before a rifle drove me off. And why, Banks would ask, didn't you tell me that long ago? I wanted to show you up. Larry grunted in disgust to himself and instead of telling the marshal, bought him a drink.

Finally, midafternoon. Larry made a compromise. He found Banks sitting at ease in his office, his feet up on his desk, anchored by the spurs on his boots. "Rest yourself, Crane. Glad you come in. I'm right weary reading them dodgers for the five hundredth time."

Larry accepted the invitation. "No trouble yesterday with the troopers," Banks said. "Besides, Rocking K wasn't around." Banks sighed. "Will be Saturday. Hope C Troop stays home."

"Four days' grace." Larry's nerves tingled as he realized Lamping in Jayhawk would be loading cattle that day. Cattle from . . . ?

"Something jigger you?" Banks asked.

"Well . . . the rustling."

"Jiggers me, too. But, shucks, there won't be none for a long time now. It's a pattern."

"Ralph, if word comes of new rustling, can you let me know first off?"

"Want to be a deputy again?"

Larry answered the lawman's grin. "Why not special deputy right now . . . for helping you chase rustlers and such?"

"Got something on your mind?"

"Deputy just for chasing rustlers when the time comes. Just a thought, but forget it."

Banks stretched an arm to a desk drawer without lowering his feet, fished for a badge, and pitched it to Larry. "Consider it done. You've already been sworn in."

Larry dropped the badge in his pocket. Banks eased deeper back in his chair. "That's only for rustling unless I tell you different."

"However you say, Ralph."

He left the office after a lazy conversation, but he hadn't told Banks about Lamping and Jayhawk. Well, when he came back from there Saturday or Sunday would be time enough—and maybe there'd be nothing to tell.

An hour later, sitting on the porch, Larry saw Matt Arnold ride by. Time passed and the shadows of the western buildings stretched across the street. The bell rang for supper and it was still daylight when Larry finished eating and returned to the porch, stood hesitant, wondering what to do. Matt Arnold mounted the steps, gave Larry a knife-look and walked into the hotel and dining room with no other recognition. His presence decided Larry. He'd go to the Brand.

He crossed the street, neared the marshal's office when a noise caused him to wheel about. Dust rose at the north end of the street from a hundred or more hoofs. Captain Darnell rode at the head of C Troop. The soldiers, in perfect formation, came on steadily and something in their grim way of riding alarmed Larry.

He stood near Banks' office. He called through the open door, "Ralph! Get out here!"

He turned to watch the advancing troopers. Darnell had now reached the upper end of the short business block. He lifted a gloved hand and gave a barked command, repeated down the line. The advancing cavalrymen split to either side of the street, though their advance did not slacken.

Banks, just behind Larry, exclaimed, "Now what is all this?"

Captain Darnell rode alone down the center of the street. People came out of stores, stood on the hotel porch, stared from the saloons. One man, venturing farther than the walk, jumped back as a heavy cavalry horse bore down on him.

Larry's eyes centered on an Army ambulance, drawn by two horses, rolling down between the double line of troopers. Darnell wheeled to face Banks and Larry. Mounted troopers, one after another, rode between the officer and the two stunned men on the porch, matched trooper for trooper on the far side of the street. Larry glimpsed Lieutenant Eaton over there; a junior lieutenant commanded the near-file.

Captain Darnell sat stiff, face frozen with a deadly fury as he watched his men ride by. When the first of them had reached the open space just this side of the station, Darnell barked commands that brought the men about to a halt, facing in toward the buildings.

Banks jumped out into the street. Instantly a trooper swung saber out of scabbard. Darnell barked, "At ease, Trooper!"

The man dropped back to position. Banks now stood spread-legged before Darnell, fists on hips. Before he could speak, Darnell said, "I have something to show you, sir, and the whole town."

The ambulance approached and Darnell signaled it to a halt. He swung out of his saddle, saying to Banks, "Come with me, sir."

Darnell walked to the ambulance. Larry made a step on the porch, but a mounted trooper glared down at him. Larry dropped back on his heels with a thud. Out in the street, Darnell had a man roll up the side tarp. Banks looked in, flinched, and his face turned pale. He wheeled to the officer. "Who did this? When?"

"I don't know who. When? I would say yesterday. These two men did not make evening muster and were missing this morning. They had been sent out on a training scout patrol." Darnell's voice lifted. "Lieutenant Eaton!"

Eaton rode up, dismounted, and saluted. "Sir?"

"Tell Mr. Banks where you found Troopers Caldwell and Brach."

"Yes, sir. Mr. Banks, my detail found them halfway between our post and Warbow, near the Rocking K line."

"And what, Lieutenant," Darnell asked tightly, "did you find near them?"

"A slaughtered beef, sir, bearing a Rocking K brand."

Larry heard the concerted gasp along the street, saw the swift exchange of horrified stares. His attention came back to Darnell as the captain said, "Both men shot in the back, their mounts picketed."

Banks looked blankly around at the double line of troopers. "But—but . . . ?"

"Caldwell and Brach were murdered, sir, by someone in or near Warbow. I brought the bodies in so that all of you can see them. You know the circumstances in which they were found."

"But I still—"

"I am giving sufficient reason for what I plan to do, sir. I shall find their killers. They are either in Warbow itself or on one of the ranches about. I

115

intend to question everyone. I have the authority, since those two men were killed while in the performance of military duty. I shall start with Warbow itself and then I shall question every man on every ranch."

"Captain, I know how you must feel about this. But you don't have the authority to—"

"Do I not, sir! I am the only recognizable legal authority between here and Great Falls. That badge of yours has no standing."

"Now wait a minute! I was hired fair and square for this job."

Darnell's lips curled under the moustache. "By a few businessmen who took the act on themselves. There was no election and there couldn't be. This is not a county. My commission outranks your badge. And I'm declaring martial law in Warbow and the surrounding territory until I find the murderers. Is that clear, sir?"

Banks' jaw dropped and his eyes bugged. Dead silence held the street. The troopers sat their mounts like statues. Larry broke the silence. "Captain, I'd like to come out if you'll permit."

"There is no need, Mr. Crane. I have the situation well in hand."

"The hell you do!" Banks exploded. "No bunch of soldiers is coming into my town and take over lock, stock and barrel while I'm wearing this badge."

"If you prevent us, Mr. Banks, you'll be the first man I'll jail. By the way, I'm taking over your office as headquarters while in town." He wheeled. "Lieutenant Eaton! Deploy the men as I ordered."

Eaton's gauntleted hand snapped to his hat brim. "Yes, sir." He turned. "Sergeants! Front and center!"

Darnell brushed by Banks, whose hand jerked up to restrain and then dropped. Face paper-white, he followed the captain to the porch of his own office. Darnell said as he walked to the door, "Mr. Crane, my compliments and will you please attend the conference?"

He disappeared inside. Banks glared at Larry without really seeing him and followed. Out in the street, the sergeants gathered before Eaton for detailed orders. Beyond the far line of immobile troopers, Larry saw the small knot on the hotel porch. Matt Arnold stood with strong hands gripping the porch rail. Larry could not see his face, shaded by the wide-brimmed hat, but the stiff tension of his body revealed enough.

When Larry stepped into the office, Darnell had placed his scabbarded sword across Banks' desk and had dropped into the marshal's chair. Darnell said, "Sit down, gentlemen. You'll need to know the procedure I've decided upon; I hope for your cooperation."

Banks lunged forward and thudded against the

desk, stiff arms supporting his shaking body as he leaned toward the officer. "Do you think you'll get one ounce of cooperation out of me or anyone in Warbow! Do you think any of us will stand for soldiers taking over the town! We're citizens, Captain, free citizens of the territory and the United States and none of us will stand for this."

Darnell's eyes glittered, but his voice remained calm. "I am aware of your status, sir. You will be free of martial law and soldiers as soon as my questioning is over. We care no more for you than you do for us."

The fury mounted and exploded in Banks. The marshal's hand dropped to his holster. Instantly, Larry's fingers clenched around the marshal's wrist and he forced hand and gun down, jamming the Colt deep into leather. Banks tried to break free, but Larry held him. His free hand blocked a wild blow, caught the swinging arm, held it. He stood chest to chest with the straining lawman, looking into the contorted face.

"Ralph! Ralph! Listen. Damn it, listen! You're crazy mad. Don't do anything foolish."

"I'll, by God, get him out of my office!"

"Ralph! Go outside and cool off. This can be settled. Let me try."

He held Banks and gradually felt some of the tension flow out of straining body and arms. Slowly, watching the man's face, Larry eased his grip, releasing arm first and then, slowly, Banks' gun hand.

Banks choked. "It's all right. I won't draw— yet."

"Try a walk. Want to leave your Colt?"

Banks' anger flared, then receded. "Thanks, you're right."

Larry asked, "Captain, will any of your men stop him?"

Darnell shrugged, caught Larry's expression, and circled the desk. At the door, he barked, "Lieutenant Eaton! Mr. Banks has permission to leave the office. He may go to any saloon. But he may not enter any other place or leave the confines of this block."

"Yes, sir."

"You've deployed the men, Lieutenant? Very good. The men will use no physical restraint unless forced?"

"They have their orders."

"Good. Return the ambulance and the bodies to the post for military burial, Lieutenant, now that the town's seen the reason for this action."

"Yes, sir."

Darnell turned back to the desk. Larry said in a low voice, "Take the walk, Ralph. Have two, three drinks. Come back when you figure you can argue sensibly."

Banks flipped the Colt from its holster and placed the weapon on the desk before Darnell.

"Just don't either of you touch it. Understand? I ain't decided how much I'm going to need it."

He stalked out. Larry walked to the door, closed it and turned, leaning against the paneling as he studied Darnell. He deliberately fell into the old Army protocol as he came to military attention. "My respects to the Captain, and may I make a suggestion?"

"Relax, Mr. Crane. There is no need for suggestions."

"Begging the Captain's pardon, sir, but you need more information about . . . the enemy? His strength has been badly underestimated."

Darnell drew up. "You presume, Mr. Crane!"

"No, sir. I know!"

Chapter XII

Larry pointed to Banks' gun. "The marshal will be back for that, Captain, and within a day everyone in Warbow will have one. You can't keep the whole town in line, I don't care how many troopers you have deployed."

"I happen to think differently, Crane."

"Can you throw a cordon around the whole town? Word will spread to the ranches and they'll be waiting for you with rifles. You're about to start a small war, Captain."

"I have declared martial law and—"

"It doesn't mean a thing. I know what C Troop has been up against. I know how you feel about the murders. But may I respectfully say that you're way out of bounds?"

Darnell's fist slammed on the desk. "I'm tired of insults and scorn, sir! I do not stand by when my men are shot in the back."

"Understood. You have declared martial law. Neither Banks nor any townsman will stand still for it. You can't ride to a ranch and arbitrarily search and question. You are not empowered."

"I am commanding officer in this area, sir!"

"C Troop had best look to its ammunition."

"We have enough—and will use it."

"I am sending a telegram to Chicago, Captain. I

shall state the full circumstances and shall ask my office to confirm the powers you claim. Word of this will get in every paper in the East. If you happen to be wrong, Captain . . ."

"You threaten me, sir?"

"I only say what is bound to happen."

The hard, bulldog set of the captain's face subtly changed, and Larry realized that the officer had acted out of accumulated tensions, his own frustration at lack of promotion, probably a nagging fear that he had been completely forgotten, and accusations of rustling—now this double murder had snapped his restraint.

"Captain, local law authority will do all it can. If it fails, then your act would probably be quite in order. But, you have not given Marshal Banks a chance."

"He is not a marshal, sir."

"If this thing came to a court, military or civilian, you might have a hard time on that point."

Larry looked out on the street. "Why not bivouac at the edge of town where you could easily know what is going on? Leave Banks to handle this. If he doesn't, then your martial law might be in order."

Larry turned, and his voice tightened. "If you don't, I shall send that wire. The railroad wants no trouble here. It does have influence. I'll leave you to think it over. Good day, sir."

He opened the door and stepped out. The troopers formed a blockade at either end of the street. Others sat their horses at strategic spots. Directly before the office, Eaton, the junior lieutenant, and a small knot of soldiers waited.

Larry met Eaton's inquiring look. "I'm joining Marshal Banks, Lieutenant. Captain's permission."

"He's at the Brand, Crane."

At the Brand, Banks stood at the bar amidst a knot of arguing men. Larry saw Nemeth among them and wondered what had brought the man to town. Banks saw Larry, pushed through the crowd, and met him. He said in a low voice, "What's that fool going to do? The bunch here is getting mad and nasty."

"Give him time, Ralph. Just a little time. Can you keep the town calm?"

"For a time, just a little time," Banks mimicked bitterly. "How long?"

"I don't know—half an hour, an hour."

"I'll try. Have a drink with me."

Larry pushed through the crowd with him. Nemeth now stood at the far end of the bar, talking with another man. He looked up and his gaze held on Larry as if registering his features. Then he resumed talking. Banks pushed a filled shot glass at Larry, and listened to the angry talk for a few moments.

He suddenly rapped his empty glass on the

bar and the sharp sound brought instant silence. "Let's smooth our feathers, gents. Might be this won't be as long and bad as we thought. I'm the man with the badge. Any move is made through me. Any of you gents decide to shoot a trooper on his own will answer to me. Unless I give the order, it's murder. Start any fights without my order and it's disturbing the peace. You'll land in jail for a week or more. Understood?"

Nemeth made a grumbling sound but subsided. Some asked, "How long do we wait around?"

"Until I've decided Darnell has had enough rope. I'm as mad as you are, so it won't be long."

The crowd moved uneasily, some ordered more drinks, all watched the batwings, and now and then some would pass a window and look out in their restless need to move.

Suddenly one of the men by the window exclaimed, "Marshal! Something's going on."

Larry moved directly behind Banks as the marshal strode quickly out on the porch. The troopers now converged at a slow pace on the marshal's office. As each group came up, Eaton gave an order and the troopers rode on to the area before the station.

"What is it?" Banks demanded.

Larry felt a surge of elation. "Let's wait and see. I think right now we should stand hitched."

Troopers rode by the saloon. Larry watched the

slow withdrawal of soldiers to the area before the station. They swiftly fell in formation; Eaton spoke briefly and then the horsemen wheeled and in tight formation rode beyond the station, railroad tracks, and pens. Eaton returned to the office and disappeared for some moments. He came out, marched to the Brand and halted, facing the curious, tense group on the porch.

"Mr. Banks. Mr. Crane. Captain Darnell requests your presence."

A few moments later, Larry and Banks faced Darnell across the desk. The officer now wore his sword at his side and only Banks' Colt lay on the desk.

Darnell spoke crisply. "Marshal, I am prepared to test what authority you have in the area. I have therefore withdrawn to a position just south of town. I am also lifting martial law. Both actions are most temporary. I shall move in again, and immediately, if I am convinced you are either doing nothing, or stalling. Am I understood?"

Banks started an angry protest, but Larry said, "Accepted, Captain. You know what this means to me."

Darnell turned to Banks. "What do you intend to do, sir?"

"Do you figure some of your soldiers can stand me long enough to take me where the men were killed?"

"They'll have orders to stand you."

"I'll take a posse and try to pick up trail. It will be old, but maybe we'll have luck. If we don't, I'll cover the ranches."

"Exactly what I planned to do."

"But they'll accept me."

Darnell said shortly, "Very well. I'll be at the hotel waiting your report, sir. Don't delay it too long."

He walked out of the office.

It was late in the day before the posse set out, Eaton riding between Larry and Banks. They could hardly do more than arrive at the murder scene before dusk, but Larry had urged against delay, uncertain as to Darnell's reaction. At dawn, the men rolled out of blankets, had coffee and a breakfast of sorts.

Eaton led the way to the dead steer. There it lay as though it had been wantonly killed for the sake of a few steaks. Banks asked Matt Arnold, who had come with the posse along with Nemeth and Bart Flynn, "Is it a Rocking K beef?"

"Brand's been cut away," Arnold answered. "But there's no ear notch and we undercut. You can't blame soldier-killing on my crew."

Flynn cut in. "Flying W don't notch but, so far as I know, I've lost no beef."

Banks made a sweeping gesture. "Spread out and find sign. That steer come from some-where."

An hour later, a posseman rode up. "Found sign

south and west, Marshal. That steer was split off from a larger drive. Main trail heads east into Rocking K."

Larry and Banks rode swiftly to the place where the trail showed plainly. The posse followed it deep into Rocking K range and then, as Larry had feared, it broke up and was lost. Wide circling failed to pick it up again and at last Banks called off the search.

He turned to Eaton. "You see what we're up against. Darnell could do no better."

"The captain won't like it," Eaton said. "But I don't know what he can say."

Matt Arnold reined about. "I'm close to home and I've been gone too long. I'll head for Rocking K."

Nemeth pushed forward. "Got some culls, Matt? If the price is right, I could buy a head or so."

"Might have. Ride along."

They split off south while the posse made the discouraged journey to Warbow. As Eaton had predicted, Darnell did not like the report. Yet he could not gainsay the word of his own officer, though he chafed for action.

Larry soothed him. "Banks won't rest, Captain."

Darnell looked at Eaton. "We could do a lot of riding for nothing, sir."

Darnell hesitated. "Very well, Mr. Banks. We'll

return to the post. Don't stretch my patience with silence, however."

By late afternoon, C Troop had evacuated Warbow and the town settled to an uneasy peace. Banks rested briefly and then saddled and rode westward with Flynn. They'd have the ranches check their ranges for missing cattle. The next morning he returned. Hampton, Flynn, the Nemeth ranch, as yet unknown to its owner, had lost beef. Sign had been found on Flying W, Banks reported. "The thieves drifted in from the north and there ain't nothing between us and the Powder. So they got half the territory to hide in between rustlings. And they're not from this part of the country."

Larry objected. "They know where the grazing beef is and know it too well to be strangers."

"Then it beats me," Banks surrendered.

"Let me do some checking on my own."

"And welcome to it! Hope you're luckier than me."

Larry went directly to the station. There would be an eastbound train through in the morning, as he had hoped. He should be in Jayhawk before noon. After supper, Larry went to the Brand and found the usual crowd at the tables and bar. The talk was mostly about Darnell's short invasion of the town and it called up anger again, offset by pleasure at the way Marshal Banks had settled it. Larry listened icily and considered returning to the hotel. Then the saddler's voice brought him up short.

". . . Rocking K shot them troopers. It figures when you remember where it happened. Right at Rocking K line."

The saddler talked with Richards and the store owner looked troubled. Then, Larry saw the young junior lieutenant, evidently in town on a liberty or perhaps, it chilled Larry, on orders.

"Don't believe it," Richards said.

"Now, figure a minute. Brand was cut off. We know Flynn and Hampton found a dead cow close to the post."

"Just guessing," Richards denied sharply.

"Well, not entirely. Blaine of Bar B—know him?"

"One of the Texans Keiler brought up three, four years ago. Homesteaded north of Rocking K."

"That'n. He was in today. Said he talked to Matt Arnold while visiting Fred Keiler. Blaine figured just what I have and he asked Arnold straight out, them being old friends. Arnold just grinned, Blaine told me, and said that Rocking K knows what to do when something happens."

"That's just . . ."

Larry didn't hear the rest. He followed the angry young lieutenant out onto the porch. His call checked the officer as he started to plunge down the steps. "That's saloon talk. Men in a small town are like old women. They gossip.

They guess and the guesses build up to look like facts. They're not."

"Perhaps," the lieutenant snapped. "But it fits in with what we know at C Troop. It also explains why your so-called lawman never tries too hard. Why should he look farther than the men of C Troop? Hell, they're the ones doing it!"

The lieutenant raced down the steps to his horse. He swung into saddle, called, "Someone needs a lesson."

He spurred northward with a roll of hoofs. Larry hurried to the marshal's office. He told Banks what had happened. Banks listened, jaw hardening.

"Too bad I can't let Darnell and Keiler tangle. That'd end two problems at once. Let's get to the Brand."

Banks slapped open the batwings and stepped into the saloon. The marshal stopped just short of the bar and waited, fists on hips, eyes glittering. A man saw him, nudged his neighbor, and soon every eye rested on Banks.

He pinned the saddler with a direct, hard look. "You talk too much. Like saying Rocking K killed those troopers."

"But I heard—"

"Damn what you heard! Do you know that feisty lieutenant was listening to every word? Do you know he's riding right now to tell Darnell?"

The saddler swallowed. "Blaine of Bar B told me—"

"Forget Blaine of Bar B—what he said and what he guessed. C Troop will be in saddle and riding to Rocking K in an hour. What kind of a massacre have you stirred up!"

He looked around. "Every one of you is deputized. Get your guns and saddle up. We ride out in fifteen minutes. If you don't like the job, blame your loose-tongued friend here and Blaine, when you get the chance. Get to your horses."

The men moved to the door. Banks strode out after them. In a matter minutes, he had covered all the saloons and the greater part of the male population of Warbow were deputies, scattering to their horses.

On the porch of the last saloon, Banks swiped his arm across his forehead. "Lord, I hope we can get to the post in time to stop Darnell."

"Not the post!" Larry exclaimed. "Ride direct to Keiler. Get there ahead of Darnell. Your posse combined with the Rocking K crew might be too much for him."

"Crane, so help me, I'm going to steal you from the railroad! I need your brains. Let's get to saddle."

Chapter XIII

Banks, Larry riding beside him, led the posse in a thundering race across the dark miles until they came close to the ranch. Then Banks called a halt. "We hope C Troop is behind us, but we can't be sure. So we'll drift in to Rocking K. If we hear shooting ahead, we'll know what it is. We'll try to break it up. We move in. No gunplay until I start it."

Banks led the way. Larry let the posse pass, then followed after. He kept ears and eyes to the rear, in the direction that C Troop would come. Free of the soft drumming of the posse's horses, he could now detect the first sounds of C Troop coming up and raced ahead to warn Banks.

But before he knew it, he came up on the shifting shadows that marked the posse. They had halted at the edge of the great area before the ranch buildings, hidden in the night ahead. He found Banks, who said, "No lights. They've gone to bed. Maybe we'd best ride in and warn 'em."

"I don't know. Suppose Darnell rides in to find Rocking K waiting for him and this posse behind him? He'd be caught two ways. I think I can make Keiler listen to me."

"Okay. We'll wait out here. Ride in and get Rocking K roused."

Larry spurred out, and the main house and buildings slowly formed out of the night. Suddenly dogs barked with a shrill, angry excitement and came racing toward him. A lamp flashed on in the bunkhouse to be snuffed out immediately. The horse danced as the barking dogs made a ring of noise about Larry, but he rode steadily to the house.

A lamp came on behind a pulled blind, to fade away, almost instantly to reappear through a window near the main door. A harsh voice came out of the darkness. "Hold it right there. Let's take a look at you."

Larry reined in. A man materialized out of the darkness and Larry saw the shadowy forms of several more behind him. "You riding in alone?"

"You can see for yourself."

"Jake! Light the lantern."

The door of the main house opened and Keiler stood framed, holding a lamp. The man beside Larry cursed in a low tone. "The damn fool! Jake, get that lantern burning."

The lantern glowed and then was held high. Larry now saw Matt Arnold with drawn gun and he could see half a dozen faces of the crew, more shadowy figures beyond the reach of light.

"Matt, who is it?" Keiler called.

"That railroad jigger, Crane."

"This time of night? Light down and come in.

But you better, by-damn, have a good reason coming around this hour."

Larry, with Arnold walking in suspicious challenge beside him, went to the house. Keiler entered ahead of him, walked to a table, and placed the lamp on it. "Say your piece, Crane."

"It's simple. Someone here hinted to Blaine that Rocking K killed two troopers and let them lay as a warning."

Keiler stared and Larry realized that, at least, he knew nothing about the rumor. Keiler caught his breath. "Matt, what'd you say to Blaine?"

"He asked if it was our beef and I said it wasn't."

Keiler demanded, "Nothing else, Matt?"

"No, except . . . I said if it had been our beef, we'd know how to protect ourselves."

"That's what came back to Warbow," Larry cut in. "Word went to C Troop and Darnell's just touchy enough to believe the story."

"Let him," Keiler said disdainfully.

"I figure Darnell's on his way here with all of C Troop."

"You come busting in the middle of the night with a cock-and-bull story like that!"

"We took it seriously enough in Warbow to make up a posse. Half the town's out there to help. I rode in ahead."

"We don't need help," Arnold sneered.

Larry turned to Keiler. "Is that sensible? You

can hold off a hundred seasoned Indian fighters? If so, I'll tell Banks and the boys to ride back to Warbow and forget it."

Keiler puffed his moustache, threw out his chest, but rocked uncertainly heel and toe. "Well . . . that many, of course . . . Won't knuckle under, anyhow, understand . . . But . . . bring your posse in, Crane. We might use 'em."

"Of course you will!" All three men turned in surprise. Carrie Keiler stood within the hall, unnoticed until now. She wore a heavy robe belted tightly about her slender waist, but it could not fully hide her rich figure. She moved forward with a sway of hips. Lamplight fell on honey-gold hair that cascaded over shoulders and down her back. Cornflower-blue eyes held concern and more than a touch of fright.

"Carrie, you git to bed. This ain't no concern of yours."

"Isn't it, Father? Do you think a stray bullet will ask who I am? Of course, you'll take the help— and use it."

In house slippers, she lost height and she seemed petite and fragile. Larry became aware that Matt Arnold practically glared at him and he tore his eyes away. But Carrie came up to him, very close.

"Thank you, Mr. Crane, for what you've done. I hope Father and Matt have already done so."

"Now look here—"

Larry broke in. "We waste time. C Troop could be moving up right now and we have to be ready for them. We're going to try to avoid a fight."

Larry explained the plan of holding the posse out of sight. They listened, Carrie with a most disturbing intentness. Arnold's dark face settled in increasingly angry and cruel lines, but he said nothing. Larry finished. "That's the plan as we see it. Do you agree? Can you send a man to Banks and tell him?"

"Send one of the boys, Matt. Git back and we'll hold more war powwow."

Matt reluctantly stepped out on the porch, barked orders, and then returned. Keiler frowned at his daughter who now sat on a sofa, robe held tightly about her, bare foot escaping from under its hem. She ignored her father and Matt who stood nearby, silent but nostrils flaring slightly and his color heightened.

Larry, feeling the tension, spoke with flat incisiveness. "Marshal Banks wants no fight with C Troop. We hope you'll help, Mr. Keiler, and that may take some doing. Captain Darnell won't be easy to talk to."

"I won't fool none with that Yankee."

Arnold added, "He comes throwing his weight around here and he'll catch a bullet."

"That's just what can't happen!" Larry exclaimed in exasperation.

Keiler demanded, "Are you telling me what to do!"

"Father! Why not let him talk? He may have a good idea and that's more than I've heard this evening."

"Now, Carrie, you just shut up and—"

"Honestly, Father! Sometimes you act as though you're afraid for someone to speak up or give advice. Are you?" Keiler's eyes bulged and he stammered incoherently. Carrie said, "Go ahead, Mr. Crane."

"We won't back down," Larry said with a thankful smile. "Darnell is no military fool, no matter how mad he gets. He'll be outnumbered and he'll back off. I'm asking you to keep tempers down long enough to give him the chance. But fight C Troop and you'll have a regiment and more to meet in a month. You—not Darnell—will be in the wrong."

Keiler questioned Arnold with a look, but the foreman only glared at Larry. Keiler pinched his moustache and lips.

Carrie swung to him and her robe parted to reveal ankles and a hem of white nightgown. "He's right, Father. Can't you keep your temper for once and order the boys to keep theirs?"

"Darnell and C Troop will soon be gone from Warbow," Larry added. "Help me get them away from here without trouble and you'll be rid of them for good."

Keiler bit his lip and then slapped his hand angrily on his knee. "All right, Crane. This time. But no one ever told me what to do before. After this, no one will again—you, my neighbors, the law, or nothing. I'll have a Texan wearing that tin badge—maybe Matt here—in six months or know the reason why. Tell Matt what you want done. We'll do it."

Arnold started to protest but saw the futility of it. Larry said easily, "Matt knows more about Rocking K than I do. He's in charge, not me. Just so there's no shooting."

Keiler jumped out of the chair. "Tell the boys, Matt. You going with him, Crane?"

Larry saw the faint shadowing of disappointment cross Carrie's face, but she said nothing. He followed Arnold out onto the porch and into the night.

Rocking K's defense was organized, men placed in strategic places where Colts and rifles could rake the yard in a hot crossfire. Arnold made Keiler and Carrie move into the cook shack. But the old man wouldn't stay with his daughter.

"She's got sense enough to keep down if bullets fly. She can handle a rifle if need be. I'll not stay cooped up like I'm scared of my shadow."

He joined Arnold and Larry, rifle in hand and gunbelt about his waist. They could only wait, though Arnold sent a rider shadowing westward in the direction attack might come. Within half an hour he came ghosting up. "C Troop, all right. Cold and dark camp about three miles out."

Larry felt a sinking of the heart. He had expected this but had hoped it might not happen. Arnold grunted an acknowledgment and they settled to wait again.

Keiler asked, "When you figure they'll show?"

"Daylight," Larry answered. "It'd be the Army way."

Slowly the night became infiltrated with a faint gray, but growing stronger. Arnold growled, peering out, "Wish they'd show."

"They'll show, don't worry," Larry answered. "Did Nemeth get his culls?"

Arnold's head snapped around. "Why do you ask? What's it your business?"

"None. Just making talk to pass the time."

"Then forget it." Arnold added grudgingly, "We couldn't make a deal so I kept the culls."

Larry said nothing, but he wondered why Arnold had volunteered information that, a moment before, had been none of Larry's business.

Off to the left and ahead a half-shadow materialized into a Rocking K puncher. "Matt, I think they're drifting in. Come back to tell you."

The light grew stronger and the ranch house materialized slowly. To the east, the sky held a faint glow and the stars swiftly faded. Then Larry saw them. At first, an uncertain, huge shadow, more like a moving line. Then, the light distorting them into high gigantic shapes the cavalrymen took form, Captain Darnell riding front and center. On either side of Larry, hidden, crouched Rocking K men stirred.

Darnell's voice ripped the dawn silence. "Troop . . . halt! Hallo, the house! Keiler!"

Larry nudged the rancher. "We'll show ourselves—you, Arnold, and me. Keep the rest down."

Keiler hitched at his gunbelt and stepped out between Larry and Matt Arnold. Darnell peered through the half light. "Crane! What in hell are you doing here?"

Keiler stepped out like a bantam cock. "Never mind him, Yankee. What the hell are *you* doing here? This is private property and you damn well know it."

"Two of my troopers have been murdered. I have reason to believe their killers are here on Rocking K. I intend to find them and take them to the post for trial, sir."

Larry intervened. "I heard the same thing, Captain. I've asked Mr. Keiler and—"

"It ain't so! Not that it's any of your business."

Darnell smiled coldly. "I intend to make it my business, sir. I can't accept the bare statement of civilians in this case."

"You'll take it, Captain, or have a donnybrook."

Darnell drew up, eyes firing. The young lieutenant appeared. He drew up before Darnell, saluted. "Sir, there is a big body of men behind us."

Larry said in a quick whisper, "Show Rocking K, Keiler. Now!"

The little man gave a roaring command. Instantly armed men appeared from around every corner. Keiler ordered, "Just hold your bullets til we find out what this jasper intends to do."

Darnell asked the lieutenant with an angry snap, "How many back there and who are they?"

"I'd say all the male population of Warbow, sir. That marshal is leading them."

"Advancing?"

"No, sir. Just waiting."

Darnell settled heavily in the saddle. He looked steadily at Larry, smiled frostily. "I'd say this is your doing, Mr. Crane. It displays quick thinking and a good sense of tactics."

"Thank you, Captain, but I'll not take all the credit. Marshal Banks can think fast, too. Mr. Keiler and Mr. Arnold here have a knack of handling fighting men."

Darnell's face tightened. "How about those killers?"

"Barroom talk blown up to be facts, and such things can happen."

Darnell did not deign to turn his head to estimate the strength of the posse behind him. He could see Rocking K's armed and waiting crew. Larry could almost read his thoughts. Darnell did not want to back down because of his officers and men. But if he didn't, he would have to explain the dead and wounded to his commanding officer, and inquiry board, and perhaps a court-martial.

Darnell's lips thinned and a muscle worked in his cheek. He finally spoke in a low, choked voice. "Lieutenant Eaton, troop will return to post."

"Yes, sir!"

His voice lifted in clipped orders that broke the formation into squads of troopers turning westward and riding slowly away. Darnell alone remained. The posse bunched some distance out, ready to attack. The body of the troopers moved out, Eaton turning back to draw rein at a respectful distance.

Darnell broke his silence. "This business is not yet ended, Mr. Keiler. And, Mr. Crane, you and I have a new problem, I believe."

He reined around with military dignity and rode without haste after his men. Lieutenant Eaton fell in beside him and they slowly caught up with the rear guard of the troop. They did not so much as glance at Banks and his posse as they passed.

Larry took a deep breath. Keiler's lips curled as he said acidly, "Could'a showed that damn Yank what Texans can do in a rumpus. But, no! I had to jump through your damn hoop! Don't know but what you'n me have a problem between us, too."

Chapter XIV

Once the posse rode in, Banks had questions that Larry answered briefly, then told him to get the details from Keiler. Carrie appeared, filled with thanks for Larry, asking him to stay at least for breakfast, but Larry refused as smoothly as he could. Carrie pouted. "I swear, Mr. Crane, you just must not like me—us."

"On the contrary." He indicated her father talking to Banks. "He's touchy right now. Maybe later . . . ?"

She looked at her father as though mentally affirming she'd bring *him* around. "I understand, Mr. Crane. He gets over mads pretty fast."

"Until then." He held her hand a moment and then hurried toward his horse.

Matt Arnold intercepted Larry, standing with hands on hips. "Crane, I've never seen anyone could bulge in on a place so fast."

"I'm sorry if I stepped on toes—"

"Now that you did! Fred's for one. And mine for another. I figure if Miss Carrie is going to listen to any man other'n her father, it'll be me."

"I have no intentions toward Miss Carrie. I'm doing a job, that's all."

"Then do your job away from here and away from Miss Carrie. I don't take at all kindly to the way you watch her and she watches you. I'll let it pass this time, but no more."

Larry made a gesture that might mean assent and moved around Arnold to his horse. The man wheeled to watch as Larry mounted, lifted the reins.

"Oh, Crane, I forgot my thanks along with the rest of 'em. That other thing held my mind."

"No thanks, Arnold, for anything—even your latest advice."

"I mean it, Crane. Never forget it."

Larry set spurs and rode fast back to Warbow, casting Arnold and Carrie Keiler out of his mind. He finally drew rein before the station, the black gelding blowing. He looked westward down the tracks and saw no sign of smoke. Just then the stationmaster sauntered out onto the platform.

"Wondered where you was, Crane. If the eastbound wasn't an hour late, you'da missed her sure."

Since he could only wait, Larry had time to sort out his impressions of the night. He realized what a close thing it had been. C Troop rifles could have ripped this range wide open. The touchy, self-trapped Captain had to have some check on him. And there was Keiler. Suddenly Larry remembered the cocky little man's statement that he'd have one of his own men wearing Marshal Banks' badge. That, Larry thought, would be almost as bad as Captain Darnell. Too bad there wasn't law of substance around here.

Larry stopped short when the idea hit him, turned on his heel and went into the station to the ticket window. "I'm sending a telegram. To Jepson Reeves, care of Gerald Marlowe, C&FWRR Land Department, Chicago. Here it goes. . . . 'Only Warbow law, a town marshal. Good man but not, repeat not, elected. His authority denied by Army and Texas ranchers who move toward violent clash. Is it possible to have a U.S. marshal or deputy marshal assigned temporarily to Warbow area? Strongly suggest such a move. Let me know. Will set my plans accordingly. Lawrence Crane.' "

Just then both men heard a distant whistle and Larry said, "Send that right away."

Larry went out on the platform and the stationmaster flagged the train. When it had slowed sufficiently, Larry swung up on the steps of the single passenger car and the train picked up speed again.

The trip to Jayhawk seemed endless, but at last Larry swung down off the train, took a few racing steps, and pulled up short just before Walling. "Lamping here?"

"Yes, but yesterday's eastbound picked up the string and the beef's well on its way east."

Larry showed his disappointment. Damn Captain Darnell and Rocking K! Larry might have been in Jayhawk sooner. Finally he shrugged. "Well, that's that. Did you see the bills of sale?"

"Lamping was upset because it was the first time I asked for 'em, but he showed 'em. I copied down the main things. In the office, Mr. Crane."

He produced rough but competent notes. The bills of sale had been for itemized head of Oxbow and Double Box. Larry's attention centered on the item: two head of Standing F, Flynn ranch, Warbow. There were other items, a head each of unknown brands. The signature at the bottom of the bill of sale was that of Joe Nemeth.

Larry's face lighted. A little bit more and he'd have proof. Walling interrupted his thoughts. "Both Lamping and Nemeth were in town yet this morning."

"Can you take me there right away?"

Once again Larry saw Jayhawk under a twilight sky. He dismounted before the hotel and Walling drove on in his buggy. Larry entered the hotel, saw no one in the lobby. He went upstairs and down the corridor to Lamping's room.

He knocked and entered. Lamping turned from a mirror where he had been combing his hair. His sallow face showed surprise and then his mouth writhed with a smile. "Well, the railroad man!"

"You've just made a shipment of beef. Could I see the bill of sale?"

"Now what's got into you railroad people! You act like I didn't have a right to ship."

"I'd just like to see the bill of sale. It is in order, isn't it?"

Lamping, with a soft oath, pulled his coat from a peg, fished in a pocket, and then held out a paper. It took but a glance to see that Walling had made a correct summary and Joe Nemeth's name had been signed in a spidery hand.

"Did this Nemeth show you his bills?" Larry asked as he returned the paper.

Lamping's eyes slid away and he turned to replace the paper. "I figured with the paper he gave me, I had nothing to worry about."

"There has been rustling in the Warbow area."

"Crane, there's rustling, more or less, on every range. I operate on a shoestring, scrounging around offseason for beef the big buyers happened to miss. I try to keep clear of stolen beef. Maybe I don't always, but if a man gives me a bill of sale ain't it enough I have a clear title so far as I know?"

Larry caught little signs of his nervousness. Lamping covertly watched for Larry's reactions, his lips in writhing motion. But Larry could not deny his argument. He asked, "Is Nemeth still in town?"

"An hour ago he was over at the saloon. Sure, he's the one you should question—not me!"

"Lamping, there's something you might like to

know. Over in Warbow, there's been just a bit too much rustling. The ranchers figure to stop it. If they catch the rustler and find who ships for him . . ."

"Don't look at me! I took everything in good faith. They can't legally touch me."

"Not legally. But have you ever tried to argue law with a man holding a Colt in one hand and a hang-rope in the other? It's something to think about."

Larry smiled and softly closed the door behind him. He hurried out of the hotel and crossed to the saloon. The moment he stepped within the batwings, he saw Nemeth seated at a table, whiskey bottle and shot glass before him. Nemeth looked up. His heavy face tightened, but then he said, "Well, well! Us Warbow folks get around. What brings you over here?"

"Cattle shipments."

"Ain't you off your range?"

"My range is wherever C&FW rails run. Part of my job is checking shipments. I'd like to talk to you about that."

Larry sat down without invitation. Nemeth grinned. "Now I don't ship. You're wasting time."

"Guy Lamping does. I've just seen the bill of sale you passed to him. None of those brands are yours."

"I buy here and there—like Rocking K culls, or a head or two from Flynn, throw in some of my own and throw my trail brands on all of 'em. Guy buys from me and he ships. So what I do ain't much of your business, is it?"

"Except your beef lands in C&FW cattle cars."

"Not mine—Lamping's by then." His eyes narrowed and his jaw thrust out. "Crane, you got nothing to do with me and let's keep it that way. I don't take to folks wandering around in my business. I've been known to do something about it."

"I see." Larry stood up and looked down into Nemeth's smiling, sardonic face. "Something like a rifle shot at me when I followed a rustling trail into hills west of here?"

"I know nothing about that. When I make a drive to Jayhawk, I go 'round those hills."

"Speaking of Warbow rustling, Nemeth, I told Lamping about it. He's nervous, seeing that Warbow ranchers just might wonder what he's shipping."

Nemeth shrugged. "Still nothing to do with me. But, speaking of Warbow, there's a lot of trouble brewing. Getting dangerous, I'd say. A man with no business over there would be smart if he stayed low—or even got out. He could get killed."

"Sounds like a threat."

"Crane, you sure surprise me! A man makes a threat, he has something to worry about. Me, I'm just a working rancher with nothing to hide. Ain't that so?"

Chapter XV

When Larry returned to Warbow, he found a telegram from Reeves. "Our Washington attorney will contact Justice Department. Can you handle situation without this action? Wire reply New York office. Reeves."

Larry wondered if Reeves hinted that the railroad could not act effectively. Or did he mean to question Larry's ability? It was the sort of two-pronged thing Reeves had thrown at him before. Larry wrote a reply. "Will handle with or without proposed action. Better with, but need to know. Shall continue with what I have until I hear to contrary." He handed it to the stationmaster. "Main New York office. Is Banks back in town?"

"Come in yesterday."

Larry walked to the land office. Gagnle arose from his desk. "I've been wondering where you were, Mr. Crane. Things are getting worse instead of better, seems like. What do you think?"

"I'll tell you later. I'm expecting a telegram from Mr. Reeves. I've told the station to give it to you if I'm not in town. I'll be at Hampton's ranch, or Flynn's with Marshal Banks. Ride out with the answer."

"Sure, Mr. Crane."

Larry walked to the marshal's office. Banks

stood by a window, his expression a study in despondency. "I'm figuring why in hell I wear the badge. Both the Army and the ranchers say it's no good and I'm beginning to believe it myself."

"Hang and rattle with it, Ralph. You just might be able to do something about the rustlers. I've been busy riding around and asking questions."

Larry told Banks about picking up the trail and following it to the hills. He told about Jayhawk and its shipments by Guy Lamping, about Joe Nemeth and his bills of sale. Banks listened with increasing excitement. "That just about wraps it up!"

"Except for catching Nemeth in the act. And we need that for actual proof."

"Why didn't you tell me about this before?"

"What could I really have told you? It would all have been guess and suspicion. Still is, for that matter, if it came to a trial."

"Sure wish we had real law in this country."

Larry hesitated and then decided not to mention his request to Reeves until he knew for certain what would happen. "I think we'd better put a watch on Nemeth's spread. He's down by Hampton and Flynn and I'm wondering if they'd help us."

"If you ride with me, we can talk to them."

"That's the way I've seen it. No time like now to ride, either."

They went first to Flying W where Larry told

what he knew about Nemeth. Hampton listened with growing concern and anger; then Banks made his proposal. Hampton said, "I agree. Let's see what Bart has to say."

Flynn, when told the news, exploded. "Nemeth! Half the time I thought so and half the time I knew I was wrong. But this sure slaps the rustler brand on him."

"Not quite," Larry warned. "We have no real proof. But we can get it if we work together."

Flynn eagerly joined in the planning. Within a short time, they had devised a scheme of constant watching of the Nemeth spread. If there was direct evidence that another rustling job was on, a rider would race to Warbow, tell Banks, who would form a posse to move in for the arrest.

Larry said, "Ralph, if you keep in sight in town, Nemeth will move more freely. But if he wonders where you are, he will stick close to home. I'll take first turn. Eric, you and Bart stay in sight, too, in case Nemeth's keeping an eye on you. The less suspicion he has, the sooner he can fall in a trap."

"But won't he be looking for you?" Flynn argued.

"He warned me to get out of Warbow. If I disappeared, Nemeth is just the man to figure he scared me off."

Larry insisted on moving out right away, though the day already waned. "Darkness can give me cover to find a good lookout place and I doubt if Nemeth or his men ride at night."

Flynn and Hampton drew a crude map of the whole area and Larry memorized it. Then, food and blankets making a saddle roll, he rode out.

The first star shone in a darkening sky and the moon made a faint silver glow as he drifted in toward the Nemeth spread. He topped a ridge and drew rein, eyes centered on the bright glow of light from a huddle of dark buildings below. He saw no movement, and the lamp light glowed steadily, peacefully. Satisfied, Larry moved slowly along the ridge. He came upon a tangle of bushes and pushed the horse into them. He broke through into a small grassy area, free of the surrounding bushes.

Larry picketed the horse and then, afoot, worked his way through the bushes to the crest of the ridge. He saw the glow of light below through a curtain of branches and leaves. Larry tried to get the layout below, but it was too dark to get more than a general idea.

The day came on, slowly brightening sky and earth. Now Larry could see the Nemeth spread. It consisted of a small main house, a few outbuildings, pens, and a single corral. Larry counted four horses in the corral. Since Nemeth worked the ranch alone with only occasionally an extra hand, Larry knew two, maybe three had drifted into the ranch. Smoke began curling from the chimney and a man came out of the house, stretched, and then looked around. Larry could hardly distinguish features, but the man's height proved he was not Nemeth. The man turned back inside after a moment.

Two hours passed. Suddenly the door below opened and four men came out. Larry instantly spotted Nemeth's powerful, chunky body. The other three gathered about him for a moment and then all roped the corralled horses and saddled them.

Larry came to a crouch. Down below, the four swung into saddle and rode off eastward at an easy pace. Larry hastily returned to his horse, pulled up picket stake, and jumped into the saddle. He emerged from the thickets and, keeping well away from the ridge, paralleled the deep swale below.

When he thought it was reasonably safe, he topped the ridge and swiftly dropped into the swale. The riders were not in sight, well ahead by now. Larry came on their trail and followed, letting the four widen distance between them and him. The trail veered to the north and held steadily.

Larry knew he rode almost on a beeline to Warbow. Within a mile, the trail changed direction again. The four men were heading directly to C Troop's post. Larry frowned, puzzled.

Why should rustlers head for the cavalry post? It came to Larry with a shock that there might be something to the rumors. Perhaps a trooper or two did help Nemeth! Larry set the horse into motion along the trail.

He climbed ridges, dropped into swales, climbed another ridge, steadily approaching C Troop, Warbow dropping away to the south and east. He topped a ridge and drew rein. The four had stopped here and, below and at a distance, Larry saw the cavalry post. Studying the sign, Larry knew the four had evidently talked for some time. He looked about to see if they had been joined by someone from the post, but there was no indication of it. The trail dropped back down the slope and continued eastward along the swale. Larry urged his mount down the slope along the trail he followed.

Soon after, he came on the Warbow road. The four had crossed it without pause and, a short distance beyond, they had turned south. Within half an hour, Larry knew he had entered Rocking K range and now he was more puzzled than ever by the four up ahead.

He pushed along, increasing his pace. He rode deeper and deeper into Rocking K. The trail veered again, pointed straight at the Rocking K ranch buildings some miles away. More puzzled than ever, Larry increased his pace.

He topped a ridge, dropped into a swale, topped

a ridge again and descended the slope. The trail now followed the swale and Larry judged he was no more than five miles from Rocking K. Men intent on cattle stealing would not venture this close to their victim's headquarters, Larry knew, so what—?

His hat jerked off his head and he heard the smack of the hidden rifle on the ridge up ahead. A second bullet split the air with a deadly scream a scant inch from his shoulder. This came from the other ridge. As Larry flinched away, he realized he had been too eager and had closed with the riders.

The first rifle smacked again and dirt splayed at the horse's hoofs. From the southern ridge behind Larry a third rifle joined in. The four must have seen him top the last ridge back there and had scattered out along both sides of this swale and waited for him.

Caught in the bottom of the canyonlike swale and four hidden rifles converged on him! Larry snapped the Colt from its holster, set spurs as he wheeled the horse. He fired at the ridge behind him where the last rifle had exploded. He saw a flash of flame and heard the bullet whip close.

Larry set the black to the ridge, snapped a shot in reply, and charged up the slope directly at the hidden rifleman.

Chapter XVI

The man on the ridge, in a panic, came to his feet, rifle lifting to his shoulder. Larry fired, saw the man flinch and then fire his rifle without aim. The bullet went wide. The men on the far ridge tried to knock Larry from the saddle when they saw their companion under direct attack. Slugs buzzed through the air, none striking the lunging target of wild-eyed horse and rider crouched low.

The man before him steadied and held his rifle to his shoulder. Larry snapped off a shot as the gelding struck the ridge top. At this short range, a rifle proved cumbersome and Larry's bullet caused the man to jerk away.

He dropped the rifle and snatched his Colt, the weapon blurring upward. Larry set spurs and the horse bore down on the rustler. Larry glimpsed a gaping mouth in a frightened face, saw the bloom of fire from the man's gun even as Larry snapped Colt muzzle down into line and pulled the trigger.

He felt a fiery finger of pain along his arm. The man fell away from the charging horse. In a thunder of hoofs, Larry whipped by. Ahead lay ridges and swales free of ambushers.

He twisted about, half expecting immediate

pursuit. But the man he had passed lay sprawled on the ground and no one else was in sight. The firing had stopped and Larry knew he had broken through.

He raced on. His arm burned, but he paid it no attention. He saw no indication of pursuing horsemen. After he had put two ridges between him and the four back there, he pulled the horse in. Then he examined his arm. The slug had cut through the cloth of coat and sleeve and gouged a shallow trough along the skin. It burned and bled, but there was no real harm.

Larry pulled his shirt from his trousers, ripped off a tail, and formed a crude bandage that he wrapped tightly about his arm. Stuffing his shirt back into his trousers and ejecting spent shells from his Colt and reloading, he considered his next move.

His slug might have found the man back there, but he had no way of knowing. In any case, they knew they were trailed and Larry's chance to follow had vanished. He rather believed they would change their plans immediately.

Larry cursed his own overeagerness. He had run into that gun trap like a green kid. He set the horse in the direction of Warbow. All the way, he watched back trail, though he began to feel more and more secure as the miles passed.

In Warbow, Banks dressed Larry's wound as he listened without comment to the story. He made final adjustments to the bandage as Larry finished and said, "Cards fell their way, not yours. Don't blame yourself."

"But if I hadn't—"

"Ifs don't brand cows or catch rustlers. Reckon they had Rocking K beef staked out?"

"That close to the house? I doubt it. Too easy to be spotted by any of the work crews."

"One thing's certain. They know you and that means Nemeth."

"They found me so far away, they'll have no suspicion the ranch is watched."

"That's right enough. But now you stay in sight in town. Flynn or Hampton can do the watching. Three men and Nemeth, eh? They're up to something and it ties in with what you learned at Jayhawk."

They sat trying to come up with an answer. Then Banks pushed himself up. "Well, I'd best put Eric or Bart on the job. I'm riding out to Flying W."

The marshal, long after dark, walked into the Brand. He saw Larry at a table and came over. He sat down, ordered a drink. "Nemeth's place is watched again. Hampton's foreman's on the job." Banks drank his whiskey, then said, "If your bullet hit that jigger, we might look for a man with a gunshot wound, if he ain't dead."

"The horse may have knocked him down as well as a bullet."

Banks suddenly asked, "You're carrying a gun, I reckon?"

"No. I don't like to."

"I wouldn't like to see you dead. Wear it on your hip from now on. Figure Nemeth knows you trailed him, and he found you snooping around Jayhawk. If he thinks you're the only one who knows about him, he'll try to shut you up."

The next day, Larry wore his gunbelt out on the street. He went to the station to find no telegram for him. He wandered to the land office to find Gagnle seated behind his desk, twirling his thumbs and looking morosely out the window.

"No telegram came for you. And I've forgotten what a land query looks like, it's been so long. Sometimes I wonder if I should stay on."

"If you want to quit, you can. Marlowe can send out another agent."

"Now, Mr. Crane, I was just discouraged, you know, but with you here I think things will change."

Larry had a touch of Gagnle's discouragement. This office had not paid for itself in months. Larry shook off the mood, stood up, and said wryly, "If you get too many customers, I'll be somewhere around."

Gagnle forced a smile. "You're not likely to be called, Mr. Crane. But thanks for the offer."

Larry walked to the Brand and had a drink. He had no one to talk to but the bartender and that soon lost its savor. He paid for his drink and walked out on the porch just in time to see Rocking K ride into town. Five riders flanked a buggy driven by Carrie Keiler. He watched her expertly handle the horses. She wore a cotton dress of subdued flower design and a straw hat covered her honey-gold hair. Larry noted the suppleness of her body as it moved with the roll of the buggy.

Then he became aware of Matt Arnold, riding slightly behind the vehicle. His black eyes stabbed hard at Larry, his lips set and thinned. Larry gave him a faint nod and turned back into the saloon.

When he emerged, the buggy stood before the general store, the Rocking K saddle horses hitched beside it. But he saw neither Carrie nor any rider. He pulled his watch from his pocket and realized the hotel would be serving the noon meal to its few guests.

He stepped into the dining room and instantly saw Carrie seated at a table. She had removed her hat, and light from the window behind her made a golden halo of her hair. She looked up and smiled. "Mr. Crane! Would it be most improper to ask you to sit with me? I never did like to eat alone. And you can tell me all about the places you've seen. I've never been anywhere but Texas and here."

"That's a lot of miles."

"But just empty miles, range country. Do sit down, Mr. Crane."

He hesitated, but she widened her smile, indicated a chair beside her, and there was no way out. He had the full impact of her eyes, subtly turned deep and violet. He became aware of curve of breasts beneath the thin cloth of the high-necked dress, of a smooth tanned arm so close he could touch it. They were served and Carrie drew from him he had been in Washington, New York, Chicago and yes—New Orleans and St. Louis. She clasped her hands. "Oh, how I wish I could see all those places!"

"You probably will, in time."

She pouted and he had never seen such a sensuous move of lips. "Not likely. I'll stay out here with Father. I guess I'll get married someday—probably to a rancher. But you've got the whole world!" Her voice held a soft, uncertain note. "Is there some girl out there that you'll . . . ?"

"No. Not yet."

Her eyes told him she was glad. Coffee finished, she sighed, "I wish this could go on, Mr. Crane, but I have to meet the boys at the store for the return home. I wish you could come out to Rocking K."

"I'd like to, but—"

"I know . . . Dad! But I'm working him around." She stood up and Larry hastily arose.

"He'll be asking you out. See me to my buggy, Mr. Crane?"

She touched his hand lightly as a signal to accompany her. They walked out on the porch. Rocking K had mounted its horses and now waited about the buggy. Carrie put her hand on his arm to descend the porch steps and did not remove it until they approached the buggy.

The punchers and Matt Arnold sat like stone, in a silence that sent a tingling warning along Larry's nerves. But Carrie walked beside him, smiling and obviously unaware of the situation. Matt's eyes glittered evilly, then hooded as Carrie came up.

She swung around to Larry. "Thank you, Mr. Crane. You have been very nice to me."

Holding Larry's hand, she climbed into the buggy, lifted the reins, gave Larry a final smile, and turned the buggy into the street. The riders moved out, without so much as a glance at Larry. He watched them roll away and disappear around a corner.

He made a disparaging sound, for himself and for Carrie Keiler. The woman must be blind to Matt Arnold's jealousy or, more likely, she could not resist putting on the charm for any man. He felt lucky that he had not been treated as Rocking K had treated that poor trooper.

Rocking K dust settled in the street. He *was* lucky, recalling Matt Arnold's dark, cruel face.

Well, done and no harm, he shrugged. He turned in at the Brand and ordered a drink. He could only wait—for Reeves' move, for Captain Darnell to flare up, for Nemeth and his shady crew to expose themselves.

The batwings batted back and Larry turned curiously. Matt Arnold advanced with long strides, eyes riveted on Larry. Larry straightened, the man's set face and jutting jaw telling him this was showdown.

Matt came to a truculent stop. He spoke in a choked voice. "I warned you."

His fist came up in a blow intended to tear off Larry's chin.

Chapter XVII

Larry jerked aside and the fist grazed along his cheek, but the blow threw Larry back against the bar. He used it as a catapult to launch himself at Arnold, who met the attack with a hard-boned knee snapping up for the groin. Larry sensed the move. The knee struck his hip as he swung half around, his fist moving with his body.

He caught Arnold in the mouth, and the foreman fell back, arms windmilling He hit a table, crashed over, and sprawled on the floor. But he came to a crouch, glaring up at Larry as blood trickled at the corner of his mouth.

The bartender yelled. "Hey, now! Not here! Not in here!"

Arnold gritted, "I'm going to tear you apart, Crane, before I kill you."

"I met her by accident and—"

The man swiped his hand across his mouth and then stared at the blood. He looked up, mad with fury. "No one does that to me, by God!"

He attacked with the surprising ferocity of a cougar. One moment he crouched by the table, the next he came in low, head a battering ram and powerful arms reaching out.

Larry had time only to fist-slam the man's head aside. But powerful shoulders slammed in hard, throwing him back against the bar. Steel fingers taloned into his side and then powerful arms circled him.

Larry's fists only bounced off hard skull and beefy shoulders even as Arnold's arms tightened in a deadly bear hug. Arnold pulled himself erect by main strength, without breaking his hug. Pain clamped around Larry's ribs. Arnold's face and jaw became exposed for a second and Larry smashed a blow into his face. Arnold's head snapped back. Larry struck with piston jabs under the arms into Arnold's sides and stomach. Arnold held a moment, then broke free. Larry bored in, not wanting to give the man respite or balance.

Arnold blocked a blow to the face, another to the ear, and several to his stomach. He steadily retreated under Larry's assault, trying to get set for a counterattack but unable to do so. His lips began to swell, but he took punishment with the stoicism of an Indian, waiting with diabolical patience for the split-second chance that Larry might accidentally give him.

Larry felt the bruising effects of Arnold's bear hug, the ache of sides and chest. Even more he felt the growing weariness of arm and leg muscles as he vainly tried to end the fight with a solid punch. Arnold merely gave ground to his attack, tried to shift away and find balance.

The two moved almost to the batwings. Larry did not let up with the high and low punches.

Arnold tried to bore in, powerful arms reaching for a deadly hug. Larry forced him back, made Arnold cover body and face. Then Larry saw a clear opening to Arnold's jaw and he snapped in a blow. Arnold spun around, stumbled into the last table before the door. His spur caught a spittoon, tipped it over, and spun it around. He caught himself against a chair but was completely exposed. Larry lunged in.

His foot struck something metallic. It spun between his feet and ankles. He could not prevent his headlong fall onto the table and it tipped in slow motion, crashed over, and he was rolled into a chair, a second one, becoming tangled, and floundered on the floor. He glimpsed the rolling spittoon that had tripped him.

A boot smashed into his shoulder, rolling him and the chair over. Arnold followed like a striking snake. His second kick caught Larry in the side, shooting pain through his body. But it also galvanized nerves to explosion.

He rolled with the next kick, reversed the roll as the boot whipped just above his head, grabbed Arnold's other leg, braced for the kick. Larry pulled savagely and Arnold fell with a sprawling thud.

Larry released the ankle as Arnold fell and rolled to his feet in a crouch, twisting to meet Arnold's attack. The man, curses bubbling the blood in his mouth, dropped his hand to his holster gun. The weapon was half out of the holster before Larry could grab the gun wrist and throw punches with his free hand.

Arnold twisted away, brought up knee into stomach in a blow that shot bile into Larry's throat. But he held desperately to the gun wrist. Arnold tried to turn the muzzle. They rolled along the floor, striking furniture, feeling nothing, bodies strained in the fury of the fight. Arnold's fingers sought Larry's eyes, but he jerked his head away.

They rolled across the floor to the far wall. Larry's head struck the heavy baseboard in a hammer blow. Lights flashed, his senses slipped, and muscles relaxed for a split second. He felt Arnold free his gun wrist, half realized the man slipped from his grip.

Then his senses cleared. He no longer held Arnold. He heard curses, shouts, thud of feet. He looked up to see Arnold thrashing in the grip of Banks, the bartender, and two other men. Banks twisted the Colt from Arnold's hand. He brought the muzzle sharply down on Arnold's skull and the man slumped.

Larry, using the wall for support, came to his feet as Banks turned. The marshal gave him a swift, searching look, whipped about to the men who held Arnold's slack body. "Get him out to his horse. Hold him. I'll be right behind you."

As they moved to the door, Banks stepped to

Larry, hard eyes inspecting him. He whirled a chair around. "Sit there, or get a drink if you need one. Don't leave this room until I'm back."

He hurried out through the batwings. Larry sat, head hanging, chest bellowing for breath. He stared dully at the floor as his lungs labored. He became aware of aching ribs, bruised knuckles, strained and knotted muscles. He felt a burn along his cheek, gingerly touched it, and realized Arnold had clawed flesh as his fingers had sought his eyes to gouge them out.

Larry looked around. Overturned chairs and tables marked the path of the fight. He looked down at stained and ripped coat sleeve, shredded shirt front. He slowly came to his feet. He winced as muscles protested.

He walked slowly and painfully to the bar, helped himself to bottle and glass. He downed the shot with a single toss, felt the tingling bite of the liquor, the slowly expanding warmth of it from stomach up through chest. He became aware of angry voices outside, looked at the batwings, took a step and then felt it wiser just to stand. He eased back against the bar.

The batwings slammed open. Banks and the bartender came in. The bartender stopped at the door to look around at the toppled furniture. Banks came up to Larry, grabbed the bottle, filled Larry's glass, and drank it himself.

"Didn't anyone tell you not to tangle with

Arnold? If he can't beat you one way, he will another. Lucky the bartender came running for me. You'd have a slug in your chest now."

Larry only gave him a long, weary look. Banks' voice softened. "Arnold's full of threats of what he'll do to you. What started it?"

"Misunderstanding."

"I know—and it's blond and it's pretty and it flirts with any good-looking stranger."

"That's right." Larry explained events leading up to the fight. "You let Arnold ride off?"

"Do you want Rocking K coming into Warbow like C Troop did?"

Larry gingerly touched his scratched face, then worked his arm to relieve sore muscles. Banks watched him a moment. "Have another drink and then get to the hotel and lie down. You need it."

Larry had his drink, then returned to his room, first begging hot water from the kitchen. He bathed off dirt and blood and poured the water over shoulders and arms. It took some of the pain away. Then he stretched out on the bed.

He awakened to find the room dark, full night outside. Someone pounded on his door. Sleep-hazed, he groped into trousers, found his way to the door, and opened it. A hard-eyed puncher insolently noted his scratched face and tousled hair. He shoved an envelope at Larry. "Miss Carrie sent this. Wish I had time to finish what Matt started, but maybe someone else will."

170

He wheeled and strode down the corridor, spurs jingling arrogantly. Larry stared dully after him, then down at the envelope. It was unaddressed. Larry stepped back into his room, lit his lamp, tore open the envelope, and read the brief message.

"Mr. Crane, I am shocked at your conduct. I would not have believed that when Matt returned for tobacco he had left at the store, he heard you boasting. About me, sir! You not only deserve the trouncing Matt gave you, but also a taste of the horsewhip. Maybe that will happen, too. Caroline Keiler."

Larry reread the note. Matt Arnold must have told a whale of story at Rocking K to explain his battered face and cut lips. The twisted version made him Carrie's gallant defender. Larry shrugged, crumpled the note, and threw it in a corner. He didn't care what Carrie, or Keiler himself thought. He was muscle-sore and hungry.

He dressed slowly and went downstairs. A lamp burned low in the lobby and the doors to the dining room stood closed. He stepped out on the porch, saw the general store was closed and dark, lights only at the saloons and marshal's office. On impulse, he crossed to the marshal's office.

"No, you can't buy anything," Banks replied to his question. "But I reckon I can rustle up some grub."

Banks lived in a couple of small rooms back of

171

his own cell block. Larry sat at a table while Banks made coffee, fried eggs, bacon, and beans. Larry wolfed down the meal, answering Banks' questions about the fight. When Larry had finished, Banks swept up plate, mug, and utensils.

"You need a drink. It'll set you up for a good night's rest, no matter how much you slept today. Come on, I'm buying."

Larry went with him to the nearest saloon, the Oxbow. There were few customers and all of them stared curiously. Banks ordered curtly and waved the man away after they were served. "They've heard about the fight. It was bound to spread all over the area. People talk."

Larry fingered the drink, took a swallow, lowered the glass, and his glance fell on the mirror. He saw the Rocking K hand who had brought the note from Carrie. The man stared in angry disgust, deliberately turned on his heel, and stalked out. Larry knew at least one source of the spreading talk. He told Banks about the note.

Banks looked concerned. "Horsewhip, huh? It's something Rocking K just might try. Keep a sharp eye, friend."

At the far end of the bar, a nondescript puncher or drifter, perhaps a rider of the shady ranges, paid for his drinks, adjusted a dusty, ragged hat and left. Banks said, "You ever considered just giving up the mess here and moving out before something else happens?"

"No! It's my job to hang and rattle and I don't like to leave a mess. Never have."

He tossed off his drink. "You were right, Ralph. Between the food and the drink, I might have a chance of living. I'm turning in."

He left Banks at the bar. He stopped on the dark porch, moved arms and shoulders, still feeling the soreness of his muscles. He slowly walked down the steps, breathing deeply of the night air. He crossed the street, started by the saddle shop.

A voice came out of the darkness of a passageway. "Crane? Crane?"

"Yes?"

Gun flame lanced orange and red, licking toward him.

Chapter XVIII

The bullet whipped off to smash a shop window across the street. Gun thunder echoed between the walls of the buildings. Larry jerked aside and his hand dropped to his holster, lifted the Colt in a flowing motion. Under the dying echoes he heard the thud of retreating boots. A shadow faintly stirred far back in the passage and Larry's gun flamed and bucked in his hand.

He heard a scream, cut off in a gurgling. He could no longer see the shadow, but he heard a thrashing about. The saloons erupted with men who had heard the roar of the shots. Banks came racing up, gun drawn.

Larry said, "Back in there, I think I hit him."

Banks moved into the passageway, Larry close behind him. They moved cautiously. They could hear nothing and the darkness was a threat. Suddenly Banks stumbled and recovered. "You downed him, all right. Strike a match."

Larry crouched beside Banks over a dark form. He struck the match and the flame revealed a man lying face down. His shirt, between his shoulder blades, showed a great dark stain. Banks turned the man over and Larry looked into the slack face of the drifter he had seen at the bar.

He had more than half expected to see the Rocking K rider. He asked, "Who is he?"

Banks answered, "I never saw him before." The match gave out. Banks checked heart, pulse, and breath, said, "He's dead."

Banks had the body carried out of the passage, across the street to the porch of his office. He brought out a lamp, held it high, and asked if anyone in the crowd knew the man. The storekeeper, Richards, said, "Seems I remember him . . . keeps ticking I've seen him . . . Wait— about four months ago! Bought cartridges and tobacco."

"Who is he? What's his name?"

"He didn't say, just that he was on his way to visit a friend he hadn't seen in a while. Joe Nemeth."

Larry and Banks exchanged glances and the marshal said, "We'll get word to Joe come morning. Right now, we'll put this one in a cell until the carpenter can build a box."

The crowd drifted off and Larry and Banks retreated to the quarters behind the cell block. The marshal said, "Nemeth. They tried to finish what they started out on the range. Now I've got a solid reason to ride out to the Nemeth spread and look around myself. I'll pick up either Eric or Bart before I ride in."

The next morning, the body was carried to the carpenter's shop and Banks rode off toward

Flying W. Larry, on Bank's insistence, pinned on a deputy badge and remained in the marshal's office. He could only sit at the desk and look through the open door onto the peaceful street. The sun climbed toward noon and Larry wondered when he would hear from Reeves. Maybe he wouldn't. He might have presumed too much. Larry reviewed the detailed reports he had made to both Reeves and Marlowe and decided he had missed no point in clearly stating the factors that had led to trouble. He had done all he could.

He heard the soft thud of a slow-moving horse just outside. Larry yawned, pulled himself up out of the chair. A bruise gave a dull twitch of pain, a muscle felt stiff. Larry realized the horse had stopped. Suddenly a man filled the doorway, stepped inside.

He might have been cowboy or rancher. Larry had a first impression of level gray eyes with a faint touch of hardness and then he saw the gold badge on the man's dusty shirt, the cartridge-studded gunbelt, and the well-oiled holster that snugged a forty-four to a muscled hip. Larry's eyes jumped back to the badge and lighted with pleased surprise as he read, "Deputy Marshal, United States."

"Glory be!"

The sharp gray eyes touched Larry's badge and he asked in a quiet, deep voice, "Where can I find Marshal Banks, Deputy?"

"He'll be back—this afternoon. Will he be glad to see you! Am I! I thought you'd come by train. Or I'd get advance word."

"Why should *you* get word, Deputy?"

"Because I'm the one who asked for you. I'm Lawrence Crane, with the Chicago and Far Western."

"Yes, you were mentioned. Unofficially, I'm supposed to talk over the Warbow trouble with you. I'm Meghan, Denny Meghan."

They shook hands. "Good to know you, Marshal, and good to have you. I'll give you the situation as it is—but, wait! You'll be hungry and they'll be serving dinner across the street. Let's eat, get you settled. By then Banks should be back. If not, I'll still line things out."

By the time they had finished eating, Larry had learned enough about Meghan to feel confident that the federal lawman would go a long way in bringing order out of Warbow's chaos. The man had official power enough. In the great number of politically unorganized areas of the West, the law centered in federal district courts and Meghan was an officer of such a court concerned with a wide area of both the Montana and Wyoming territories.

But personal revelations about Meghan himself pleased Larry and gave him more encouragement. He had ridden hundreds of miles directly cross-country, to arrive in

Warbow far sooner than the circuitous, torturous route of the railroads would have allowed him to.

"What your railroad needs, Crane, is short north-south connecting lines. From Missoula to Minneapolis and back to Warbow, changing trains at least twice!"

"The connecting lines will come as soon as the country settles up. And that depends on bringing law and peace to places like Warbow."

"Let's talk about that—over at the marshal's office?"

Larry outlined the situation as it had developed. Meghan asked questions now and then. The discussion had not been completed when Marshal Banks strode in, clothes dusty and face alight. But he froze when he saw the stranger, until the man turned around and he saw the golden badge. "Larry! He's come!"

"Meet Denny Meghan, Ralph Banks."

They shook hands as Larry explained that he and Meghan had reviewed all Warbow's problems. Banks said soberly, "Not quite all, Larry. I went to the Nemeth spread and he said he had no friend in Warbow. But he had two riders with him. Never saw them before and they claimed to have come from Powder River country, a long piece from here. Joe claimed they were distant cousins from up that way."

"Were they?" Larry asked.

"How could I prove it without going to Powder River?"

"Three men rode with Nemeth the day I trailed them. I shot that man last night and now there are two. So we have a good idea that Nemeth lied about the dead man."

"But they'll not make any new tries for a while, Larry. You can ride and walk safe. Point is, what are they planning up there at Joe's? You told Meghan about our patrol?"

"He did," Meghan answered. "What have been the movements of Nemeth especially, and of these three men?"

Larry traced them, from his meeting with Lamping back to Warbow, the ride toward Jayhawk, and then the shooting last night. He finished, speaking to Banks, "That man last night knew me from looking at me over a rifle sight. They decided to cut me down."

Meghan hitched at his gunbelt. "I'd say you ruined some plan, probably a cattle theft, when you trailed 'em. You got out of the ambush so they played safe—just forgot the plan and went back home. But there's some pressure on 'em. They tried to take you out again last night but failed. You'll have action soon. Maybe I'd best get in the picture right away."

"I'll ride you to Flying W and the Nemeth spread," Banks offered. "Now, if you like."

"I would. Crane, you coming along?"

It was near dusk when the three rode into Flying W. Lamps glowed from the windows and Eric came out. "I say, Ralph! Back so soon! Something up?"

Banks introduced Meghan and Hampton gave an exclamation of delight when Ralph explained the federal man's authority. "Now that is top hole. Between Texans, troopers, and rustlers we've had a bloody old time, y'know."

He saw Larry and his warmth departed. "Mr. Crane. I assume business brings you."

"Otherwise I'm not welcome?"

"Well, Mrs. Hampton and my daughter have heard of that unfortunate fight. Can't say I approve of its reason."

Meghan said dryly, "What has this to do with rustling? Let's get on with that and afterwards you can settle your personal differences. I want to be looking at this Nemeth ranch come dawn."

Hampton said, "Of course. We're just eating. Join us?"

Larry hesitated, but Meghan said, "I'd appreciate it."

Mrs. Hampton and Evelyn greeted Banks warmly, graciously made Meghan welcome, and looked distantly at Larry. Banks blurted, "You heard a twisted story, ladies."

"Ralph, I can speak for myself—that is, if they wish me to."

Mrs. Hampton nodded distantly; Evelyn, when

Larry looked at her, flushed and her eyes slid away. She said in a muffled voice, "It's only right, Mr. Crane. I assume you do have a side."

Larry started to speak, then looked at Mrs. Hampton, sensed the rigidity of tradition, sensed under the pleasant and apparently normal warmth of the woman, a stern code, probably based on her own prejudgment of any situation. Evelyn, lovely, younger, softer, watched him with the same cold withdrawal, and her father stood impatiently, wishing this thing over and Larry gone.

Larry said slowly, "I've changed my mind. Perhaps Marshal Banks should speak for me. He'll be more acceptable. Thanks for your offer, Mr. Hampton, but I'm not really hungry. Ladies . . . good night."

He gave them a curt bob of the head and walked out in a dead silence. He moved aimlessly about in the night.

The house stood solid, the windows aglow, but now the light no longer inviting. He thought of Evelyn and then of the half-formed dreams he had. In a very real sense these last embarrassing moments had told him much about the Hamptons, and Evelyn, that he might never have discovered or, had he carried out his dreams, discovered too late. Trust, he felt, was something that sprang spontaneously between people.

Three men came out. Larry moved forward to

meet them. Hampton said uncertainly, "Y'know, Crane, stories can sound real and true enough."

"Shall we forget it? We have to do some riding."

"And the sooner the better," Meghan added.

Hampton led the way, taking another Flying W man with him. They found the watcher overlooking Nemeth's ranch. They held a conference, Meghan doing most of the talking. Hampton and his men rode off. Banks, Larry, and Meghan rolled up in blankets.

Before dawn they were awake and in position. Full day came. Nemeth and his two friends moved in and out of the buildings occasionally but nothing more. The sun climbed higher. Meghan suddenly pointed off to the west. "Who's that?"

The rider coming down the swale looked familiar, even at this distance. Then, as he approached the house and Nemeth and his friends came out, the rider brushed his hat back from his face.

Larry and Banks softly exclaimed at the same time, "Matt Arnold!"

Chapter XIX

They watched Arnold dismount and walk into the house with the other men. They did not emerge for almost an hour. Then Nemeth and his two friends saddled their horses while Arnold waited. All of them rode off down the swale, retracing Arnold's route.

Meghan said, "Maybe this is what we've hoped for."

"But Arnold?" Banks demanded.

"We won't waste time guessing. Let's find out."

They returned to their horses. The experienced Meghan cautioned against pressing too closely on the cavalcade now far ahead. They headed directly west, angled north and crossed the Warbow road. In a short time, Banks said, "Rocking K range."

Soon the trail angled south as though heading directly toward the ranch headquarters. Meghan drew rein and studied the trail. "They'll be not too far ahead. Maybe we'd best split up. Give me five minutes and then follow."

He moved ahead along the trail. Banks and Larry waited and then followed after. They moved at a slow pace. Less than two miles along, they saw Meghan riding back to them. They joined him and he pointed back toward a ridge.

"Just over there. There's a bunch of beef I'd say they're readying to drive. Maybe you two had best take a look."

They followed him along the base of the ridge. Larry saw where Nemeth, Arnold, and the two men suddenly turned up the slope. Meghan drew rein. "Ground-tie your horse. Follow me and keep your hands close to your guns."

They climbed almost to the top of the ridge. Meghan crouched down, signaled Larry and Banks to follow suit. They crawled the remaining few yards, removed their hats, and slowly lifted their heads.

The four men they had followed worked at least twenty head of beef. Matt Arnold indicated one of the steers and cut it away from the herd. Nemeth and one of his friends started moving the remainder of the beef eastward. Arnold and the other choused the single cow west and north.

Larry dropped back below the ridge with Banks and Meghan. Banks said, "Splitting up? What do we do now?"

"Follow the main herd," Meghan answered.

"Wait," Larry checked them. "Let's trail Arnold and that other rider. Why did they cut out that one cow? Where are they taking it? Not to Rocking K, that's sure."

Banks slapped his knee. "C Troop! Do you reckon that's . . . ? Sure! He's right, Marshal."

"You two should know more about guessing in these parts than I do. Follow the single beef."

They swung into saddle, making a wide circle until they picked up sign of the single beef and the two riders. Larry suggested they follow close. "Arnold and the other rider won't expect trouble. And a single steer can keep two men busy."

"Right enough," Banks agreed.

Twice they found where the beef had tried to cut back to the main herd. They neared C Troop's camp. The three drew rein when they heard a single gunshot ahead. They searched the ridge, but no one appeared. Meghan said, "We'll spread out—wide. Keep low and watch. So far, they haven't done a damn thing we can arrest 'em for. You say that's the Rocking K foreman up ahead?"

"And a Rocking K beef," Larry added.

"So what can we do? Ride out now to either side and we'll drift ahead."

Larry raced westward until Meghan, holding center, was hardly more than a dot, then he turned to the north and rode up the ridge. Far over to his right, he saw two small figures, two horses and an unmoving shape on the ground that could only be the steer. Larry paralleled the ridge, then dismounted and crawled to its crest.

Now Matt Arnold, and the second man were directly below him and a short distance out. The rider, kneeling beside the beef, worked while Matt Arnold stood over him. The rider came to his feet. He had cut off a haunch. Both men turned to their horses, cursed them as they shied at the smell of fresh blood. Arnold said something and the two men rode at an angle down the swale, abandoning the slaughtered steer.

Larry moved back to his horse and mounted. He drifted along the base of the ridge toward Meghan. He saw the marshal, waiting beside his horse. Far beyond him, Banks came riding to join them.

Banks reported. "They rode by me. I figure they're joining up with the others."

"Crane, what did you see?"

Larry told them. Banks swore. "So that's why C Troop's been blamed! They will this time unless we move in and—"

"What?" Meghan asked reasonably. "Rocking K beef, and Rocking K foreman ordered the steer shot. He'll come up with a good reason for it if we jump him."

"But it's plain—!"

"A steer shot, left lying on order. What else is plain?" He let it sink in. "No need to trail these two. They'll join the others. We can make a wide circle and pick up the main bunch."

They returned to the place where the cattle had been bunched and the trail lay plainly before them, heading almost due east. They followed it for several miles and then Meghan rode ahead to scout. He soon returned. "A mile or so ahead. But there's only three riders now. One dropped off somewhere."

"Playing rear guard?" Larry asked.

"Don't think so. He'd have picked us up by now and warned that bunch ahead. They're riding slow and easy."

"Nemeth with them?"

"The stocky one? Him and the other two."

"So Matt Arnold left them. He'll be riding home. All we can do is watch Nemeth."

They trailed the slow-moving herd. At dusk when Banks knew the beef would be bedded down, the three men scouted cautiously forward. They finally saw the flicker of a fire ahead and drifted closer. Nemeth and a man sat in its light. Out beyond, Larry heard an off-key voice singing to keep the beef grazing and sleeping.

After a brief, whispered conference, Banks and Meghan faded back, taking Larry's horse, to make a distant camp. He worked his way up a small slope and dropped prone in the high grass at its crest. Dawn found Larry watching the stirring camp below. The fire was stirred up and Nemeth and the other two produced straight-irons, that necessary tool of the rustler.

The men ate while the irons heated and then Nemeth and a rider rode to the herd, neatly cut a beef away and drove it to the fire. Instantly it was roped and the third man worked the iron over the brand on the flank. It was released, driven off, and the process repeated.

Larry dropped back down the slope and hurried in the direction from which Banks and Meghan would appear. Within ten minutes he saw them ahead, leading his gelding. He told them what happened.

"Brand changing," Banks and Meghan said as one, and Meghan asked, "Where will they drive them?"

"Jayhawk station," Larry answered instantly. He studied the sun, judging the time. "We can be in Warbow in time to catch the eastbound. We'll be in Jayhawk station late tonight. Plenty of time to set your plans, Marshal."

Meghan instantly agreed.

That night they descended from the train at Jayhawk station. Walling stared hard at Banks and Meghan until Larry identified them. Larry asked, "Have you a request for cattle cars?"

"Two—day after tomorrow. Guy Lamping asked for 'em. Funny thing, he acted like he was scared of his own shadow and I thought he'd change his mind two or three times. But he didn't."

"He's in town?"

"Come in a week ago. At the hotel. Speaking of hotels, I'll ride you gents in—"

"No," Meghan cut in. "We don't want to be

seen. We can spread blankets in the baggage room. Oh, and bring some chow back from town come morning."

They camped fairly comfortably in the locked and empty baggage room. Early the next morning Walling came in with food. Mid-morning, they heard the westbound approach. Some distance beyond the station it slowed and then they heard increasing sound. Larry explained, "Backing onto the spur line before the pens. It'll be dropping off the empty cattle cars."

At last the train pulled out west and all was silence. A few minutes later, Walling knocked on the door. "Lamping's coming down the road."

They heard muffled voices for a time and then silence, unbroken until Walling threw open the door. "Won't be anyone around now until tonight's westbound. Lamping's going back to town, so stretch your legs."

Larry asked, "Did Lamping say where his shipment was coming from?"

"West. Same gent he's dealt with before."

"Nemeth!"

"He said beef would be loaded so tomorrow's eastbound can pick it up."

They could only wait. Walling brought food the next morning. They had no more than finished eating when Walling hurried in to warn them that Lamping was coming down the road. Shortly thereafter they heard a querulous, nervous voice lifted in brief argument and then silence. Time passed.

Then they heard a distant lowing and that slowly increased. A small herd passed close to the station. There were high yipping sounds as men choused the cattle along. A bull voice roared, "Open that pen!"

"Nemeth," Banks said.

They could tell that the cattle had been penned beside the cars and, soon after, they heard the process of loading begin. Suddenly steps sounded outside the door and Walling said in a loud voice, "Sure, Lamping, you'll get your manifest. But you know the new rule and—"

"Bill of sale. I know!"

Meghan sent a silent signal to Larry and Banks. He silently inserted the key in the lock, grimaced with the effort to throw it without a click. The whisper of sound was covered by Lamping saying, "Damn nuisance. Before, there was none of this showing bills of sale. Anything, I suppose, to hold a man up and—"

He broke off when Meghan stepped into the waiting room, Larry and Banks close behind him. Lamping saw first, the golden federal badge and then he saw Bank's nickel one. His jaw dropped, liver lips worked at his eyes bugged.

Meghan held out a hand. "I'll see that bill. Deputy federal marshal for this district, Lamping."

Lamping stared at Meghan and slowly extended

the paper as though hypnotized. Meghan looked at it, read aloud, "Twenty head Circle-in-Star brand. Owner, Joseph Nemeth." He looked up at Lamping. "Fresh brands?"

"I . . . I didn't look. Been all right before and—"

"In there," Meghan jerked a thumb toward the baggage room.

"You can't arrest me! I—"

"In there, Lamping. Now you wouldn't want to resist a U.S. marshal, would you?"

Lamping moved to the door, protesting, "I've done nothing. So far as I know, Nemeth's just a drover from Warbow way. I had that bill and—"

Meghan closed the door on his protests, locked it, and said to Banks and Larry, "Help me make arrests. Watch sharp and move fast, if it comes to that."

On the spur line, Larry saw cattle going into the last car and he glimpsed men forcing them up the loading chute. He made sure that his Colt would slide easily out of the holster as he walked toward the cars. Rounding the end of them, he saw just two steers left in the pen. Nemeth and his riders did not see the lawmen as Meghan swung open the pen gate and stepped inside. The two animals lurched up the chute at that moment, Nemeth and his friends closed the car door. Wiping his face with the back of his hand, Nemeth turned and froze.

Muddy eyes jumped to Banks, to Larry, then back to Meghan's gold badge. Meghan said, "I'll look at those brands, Nemeth. We watched you use running irons back on Rocking K."

One of the men took a step as though to climb over the chute. Meghan snapped, "Hold it!"

The man froze. Meghan approached the lower end of the chute. Larry and Banks moved out to either side behind him. Then Nemeth's hand slashed to his gun. His friends dropped to a crouch as they tried for their weapons.

Meghan's Colt blasted and one of the riders pitched forward, gun spilling from his hand. Nemeth had freed his weapon, but Larry's slug caught him in the right shoulder, slamming him back against the car. The third man threw away his Colt, jerked erect with hands high.

Meghan growled, "Open the door. Larry, check Nemeth and the other jasper."

The fallen man was dead and Nemeth's right arm hung useless, blood oozing through his fingers as he clutched the wound. Larry kicked three guns aside and forced Nemeth to stumble down the chute into the pen. Meghan came up to Nemeth, who looked glaze-eyed with shock. "Matt Arnold helped you. We saw that. We have Lamping locked up in the station. Do—"

"I'm shot, damn you! Are you going to let me bleed to death!"

"Depends on how quick you tell us why Matt Arnold worked with you."

Nemeth saw Meghan's firm-set jaw and steely eyes. "I'll tell you. I'll tell you! But for God's sake—!"

"Get him to the station," Meghan cut in.

Within fifteen minutes, Nemeth, Lamping, and the other man told their stories while Nemeth's wound was bandaged. Larry said, "We'd better get to Rocking K. Now we know why that beef was left up by C Troop. There could be a lot of trouble."

Meghan asked Banks, "Can you hold these prisoners here? We'll get 'em to your jail later."

On Banks' nod, Meghan said, "Crane, let's get west in a hurry."

Chapter XX

Walling drove Larry and Meghan to Jayhawk, where Meghan commandeered saddled horses. They raced westward. Night caught them just this side of the hills and, on Larry's advice, Meghan reluctantly agreed that they might lose their way in the tangle of swales and canyons.

They tried to sleep but had scant luck. The next morning they mounted and ate up the westward miles after threading the torturous hills and finally breaking free. They soon came to a point where Larry reined in and Meghan drew up beside him. Larry pointed south. "Rocking K ranch house should be off in that direction, maybe five, ten miles. Not far up ahead is where Matt Arnold left Nemeth."

"Let's ride in after him," Meghan said flatly.

"What if we hit some Rocking K work crews?"

Meghan touched his badge. "Unless they've thrown in with him on this deal, they'll do nothing."

Both men kept a sharp eye for a glimpse of a Rocking K hand or work crew, but as the miles rolled by, they saw only a few head of beef. At last they topped a swale and Larry pointed down at the sprawling Rocking K complex.

Meghan's brow lifted. "Big enough, for sure. But it's deserted as though everyone rode off to a picnic or a spree on the town."

The two men moved down the slope. They expected to be seen at any moment. But nothing moved. They wound their way through corrals and outbuildings. No one appeared; no one called a challenge. All the corrals were empty of horses and there was only silence from the great barn. Larry felt something like fear, as though he instinctively knew the unexpected had happened.

Meghan pulled up. "I don't like this. By now we should've seen someone!"

"But where would they go—all at once and together?"

Meghan indicated the house with a move of chin. They rode toward it, hands close to holsters. They were almost to the house, when the rear door opened. Carrie Keiler stepped out, a heavy Colt in her hand that she lined on them. "That's just far enough. Mr. Crane, I'm surprised you have the nerve to show your face here. What do you want?"

Meghan said, "I'm a deputy U.S. marshal, m'am. I'd like to talk to Matt Arnold."

Carrie's lips curled in disgust as she glanced at Larry. "Do you actually mean to have Matt arrested for defending my name against your loose tongue?"

Meghan cut in. "I want to talk to Arnold, m'am.

It has nothing to do with you. This is serious government business."

"He's not here." Carrie moved the gun muzzle a trifle. "Why don't you ride on?"

Meghan smiled frostily. "Lady, you may be telling gospel truth, but I have to see for myself that he's gone. I intend to come in and look around. Interfering with a U.S. peace officer in pursuit of his duties could put you in jail for a few years, seeing that it might also be aiding a criminal to escape."

"Criminal! Matt? What in the world do you think he's done?"

"Rustling, m'am. Your spread just lost twenty head of beef and—"

"Are you crazy! Why . . . why, just yesterday Matt found rustler signs he trailed to C Troop, those thieving Yankees! He saw troopers cutting up a beef they had killed. The rest they had driven north."

She forgot to hold the gun on them, stepping out from the door. "It's true. Matt told Dad and Dad decided it was time to catch those rustlers red-handed even if he had to ride through that camp."

Larry demanded, "Is that where—"

"Of course it is. You'll see who's the rustler when Rocking K tears off the lid!"

Larry forced himself to calmness. "When did they leave?"

"Maybe two hours ago. Matt sent riders to call in every hand from the range."

"Can you stop it, Meghan?" Larry asked in a cold sweat. "Arnold's set up a massacre."

"I'll have to stop it. Which way's the camp?"

Both men rocketed out of the yard and Larry headed north and west. The miles sped by, empty miles that dashed hope they might catch up with Rocking K. They came to the Warbow road and the horses' hoofs drummed northward. Larry momentarily expected to hear the sound of a battle ahead. He recognized the high ridge, just beyond which lay C Troop's camp. He shouted the information to Meghan.

The marshal signaled a halt. As the horses blew, he studied the ridge. "No shots. No riders. No troopers. It's not started yet. There's not time to get a posse so . . . just you and me. We'll see what's happening and"—he shrugged—"and work with what we see."

They moved swiftly up the slope. They topped it and looked down on the post. Over to the right, a blue line of troopers faced the armed Rocking K riders. Larry saw too many punchers even for Rocking K. Keiler must have sent fast word to his Texas friends and they had gathered with their crews. The cavalrymen formed a firm blue line, controlled and so far restrained. The cowboys looked like a rabble, but Larry knew they were as much fighting men in their way as the troopers.

Just visible between them, Larry saw Captain Darnell and his officers facing Fred Keiler and Matt Arnold. Keiler made an angry sweeping gesture. Larry said, "Any little thing can start that down there."

"Even us," Meghan agreed. "But we have to do it. I'll do the talking, but keep your eye on Arnold. He won't know about Nemeth and Jayhawk. I'll make the arrest after I've got those soldiers and punchers calmed down. But watch him all the time."

The two men set spurs and raced down the slope. There was a faint ripple along the blue line, but discipline held them firm. The punchers pointed and shouted. Fred Keiler and Arnold looked up, startled, and reined their mounts around to face the new element in the tense situation. Half a dozen punchers spurred out to meet Larry and Meghan.

They fanned out to block them. Larry and Meghan continued down the slope and across the swale. One of the punchers saw Meghan's badge, slowed his pace, and the others followed. Larry noted their hands remained close to holsters.

Meghan finally drew rein. "What the hell are you people trying to do!"

"Getting us a bunch of rustlers. Who are you?"

"United States marshal, friend. If anyone is going to get rustlers, I'll be the one to do it. Stand aside."

He moved forward, Larry beside him. The Texans reined aside, letting Larry and Meghan through. They fell in behind them. Captain Darnell and Lieutenant Eaton had fully reined about. Keiler and Arnold exchanged puzzled glances. Meghan's hard glance rested on Keiler, Arnold, then swept the bunched Texans beyond. He looked hard at Captain Darnell.

He introduced himself in clipped words and Larry noted the surprise and consternation in Fred Keiler's face. Meghan continued speaking to Darnell. "I am not aware, Captain, of civil war, riot, or general lawlessness in this territory that warrants calling out your command."

Darnell's face grew choleric. He glanced at the golden badge and managed to speak levelly. "I was not aware, Marshal, you were in the area."

"You are now, sir. We have no need, as yet, of your men. Dismiss them, Captain, if you please."

Darnell blazed. "We're accused of rustling, sir!"

"Who brings the accusation, Captain?"

Keiler spoke truculently. "I do. And, by God, I have the proof."

"Are those your friends back there?"

"You bet they are and we intend to see that we get justice. No sneaking Yankee is going to run off my beef and—"

"Justice you'll get, sir." Meghan stabbed a finger at Keiler, Darnell, Arnold, and Eaton. "You four—that's all. I guess I can get both sides of the story from you. Send your friends home, Mr. Keiler. Captain, dismiss your men."

Darnell's nostrils pinched white and his moustache bristled. But he recognized the change that Meghan's presence made. He spoke in a tight voice. "Lieutenant, dismiss the troop. Hold them in readiness within the post. Then attend me."

Meghan asked, "Mr. Keiler?" as Eaton rode away and his voice lifted in sharp commands.

"Be damned if—"

Meghan's gun blurred out and Keiler looked into its black muzzle. Arnold's hand dropped to his holster, but Larry warned, "Don't try it."

He held his Colt on the foreman, who snatched away his hand, glowered murder. Meghan said quietly, "You head a mob, Mr. Keiler, nothing more. Keep yourself and them out of trouble. Send them home. Now."

Keiler fumed, snorted through his moustache but finally snapped, "Matt, take 'em back to Rocking K. But hold them ready."

Meghan said, "Just a minute. Who witnessed the rustling?"

"Matt did."

"Then Mr. Arnold had better stay with us. You can tell your friends to go home, right from where you sit, Mr. Keiler."

Keiler glared but beckoned a man to him. They

conferred, Keiler made a gesture, and the man returned to the main group. In a few moments, the Texans rode slowly down the swale and finally disappeared.

Meghan holstered his gun, but threw a warning look at Larry, a flick of the eyes to Arnold. Larry replaced his Colt and Meghan said, "All right, Mr. Keiler. You're the accuser. You'll speak first. Captain, if you please, no interruptions. You'll have your defense in full."

Keiler heatedly told the story. "Matt saw that steer haunch brought right into this post! Three troopers. They've run the rest of the beef off—nigh twenty head and that's a lot of money to add to their monthly pay."

"You saw all of this, Arnold?" Meghan asked. Larry moved slightly to have a clear line on Arnold. The foreman agreed, with curses.

Darnell made an angry sound, but Meghan listened attentively until Arnold finished with another curse flung at the captain. The marshal's hand dropped casually to his side, hand just below his holster.

"Would you swear to that in court, Arnold?"

"To every damn word!"

"Then you'd be in trouble. I've just come from Jayhawk station where a man named Nemeth tried to load rebranded Rocking K beef onto cars. I'm holding him and a crooked buyer named Lamping along with another man—

Nemeth's rider. The second stopped a slug."

Larry, watching Arnold, saw the quick play of expression across the dark face, the sudden fear that filled the eyes.

Meghan said, "Joe Nemeth talked—about the stolen beef and about the one you, Matt Arnold, helped drive over here and—"

Arnold's hand blurred down and Meghan, a split second late, grabbed for his gun. Larry slashed hand to his holster at Arnold's sudden blaze of eyes preceding by a breath his move to his gun. Both his and Larry's Colts roared as one. His slug smashed into Arnold's side. The bullet sang close over Meghan's head and then the marshal fired.

Arnold was flung from the saddle by the double impact. Keiler and Darnell sat like stones, eyes bugged and rounded. Larry jumped to Arnold's side. The man lay with eyes closed. Larry's slug had grazed the man's side, but Meghan's had smashed high on a shoulder. Larry called, "Alive. Needs patching. He'll stand trial."

Meghan asked Darnell, "You have a dispensary?"

Darnell recovered. He said to Eaton, who had ridden up, "Get our medics, Lieutenant. On the double!"

Eaton raced for the camp. Keiler caught his breath and blazed at Meghan. "What is the meaning of this! That's my foreman and—"

"He was robbing you, Mr. Keiler. Captain Darnell, can we settle this business in your office as soon as Arnold is moved?"

Not long after in Darnell's inner office, Larry watched Keiler's confidence crumble as Meghan told the story. At first the little Texan bubbled angrily. But gradually he sat silent, hands clasped tightly. He shook his head in disbelief. "You mean Matt figured this all out? He gave my beef to Nemeth? Why he stole from his best friend, me!"

"Stealing was just a way to his real plan," Larry said. "You and Captain Darnell locked horns. Arnold had ambition. He wanted Rocking K and he wanted your daughter. He drove off those who caught her interest, but he was afraid of one thing."

Keiler tugged at his moustache. "But—but Matt didn't need to do that! He'd always be my foreman and even if Carrie married someone else—"

"That's the *if* that caused the trouble. He figured you'd want her to marry a rancher, not a hired hand. In fact, Miss Carrie herself thought that's the way it would be. She said as much. So, Matt helped Nemeth steal your cows and put the blame on C Troop. He built up your anger against the soldiers and he kept trouble boiling in Warbow. Sooner or later, he knew you and the captain would have a showdown. It nearly came at your own ranch."

"But that's what I don't understand! Why—"

"You could be killed, Keiler. Soldier's bullet or Arnold's would make no difference. C Troop would have the blame."

Keiler stared. "You *know* all this? You know for dead certain?"

"Nemeth told us in Jayhawk and his rider and Guy Lamping confirmed it. You saw what Arnold did when we called him on his story. As a last resort, he'd have bushwhacked you, and the soldiers would have been blamed."

Keiler's fist beat on the arm of his chair. "Why? Why?"

Larry explained. "He'd run Rocking K. Miss Carrie would turn to him and he'd pressure her to marry him. He would *be* Rocking K then."

Meghan's voice sharpened. "Arnold's done working for anyone but the government in a penitentiary for a long time. So you'd best look for another foreman. There's something else. I'll make sure you understand and then we'll be done with it."

The marshal tapped his badge. "*This* is the law, Mr. Keiler, until Warbow's large enough to have a sheriff. Then *he'll* be the law. If you have trouble, come to me and not to your friends, Texans or otherwise. Is that understood?"

Meghan turned to Darnell. "Captain, your martial law may have had a faint shadow of legality, considering there was no law. But there is now. I believe we understand one another."

"We do, sir."

Larry studied the officer and the rancher. "You both fell in the same trap, gentlemen. You both acted honestly as you saw the situation. Why not shake hands and end the matter?"

Darnell sat ramrod straight and forbidding, glaring down his nose at Keiler who puffed through his moustache. The little rancher slowly stood up. "I reckon I should thank you, Crane. But hearing this about Matt—"

"I know. Forget the thanks. What about Captain Darnell?"

Keiler shoved his hat on his head. "I may have to live with him, Crane, but I sure as hell don't have to like him. He keeps to his range, I'll keep to mine. I reckon I better head for home. Carrie will be wondering."

He strode out in a dead silence.

Later that day, Larry sent a telegram to Reeves, copy to Marlowe. "Thanks for U.S. marshal. Rustlers arrested. C Troop and ranchers will keep peace. Do I stay in Warbow? Lawrence E. Crane."

After supper, he went to the Brand. Meghan had left for Jayhawk to pick up his prisoners to take them to the district federal court for arraignment and jail. Arnold would be transferred as soon as he could be moved from C Troop's dispensary.

Word had already spread about the rustlers, the

arrests, and Arnold's part in it. Excited talk rippled along the bar as Larry came up. He ordered a drink, listening, evading eager questions. Suddenly Eric Hampton appeared beside him. He grinned, abashed, hesitated, and then blurted, "I say, do have a drink with me. I made a bloody ass of myself, what!"

"Thanks, I'll take the drink. Don't be too hard on yourself. Darnell and Keiler were fooled, too."

They had a drink. Hampton hesitated, then blurted, "My wife and Evelyn . . . asked me to convey best regards and all that. Evelyn is especially upset."

"She needn't be. Will Lieutenant Eaton be visiting you soon?"

"Matter of fact, tomorrow night, I believe."

"To borrow from you Englishmen . . . top hole, that one. Good night, Eric."

The next day Larry loafed in the land office where Harvey Gagnle excitedly wrote letters to prospects and answered queries that had stacked up over the months. He effusively thanked Larry, repeated the thanks, until, at last, Larry picked up his hat.

The stationmaster, breathless, filled the doorway. "Any soldiers in town?"

"At the Oxbow," Larry answered. "I saw a sergeant and a couple of troopers."

"Thanks." The man turned, whirled around. "Know what?" He shook a flimsy. "Telegram from Washington. War Department! C Troop ordered back to Great Falls. And here! Another! Captain Darnell—he's a major! Going to San Francisco! The Presidio—whatever that is."

He darted away. Larry and Harve stared at one another and then whipped about when the stationmaster suddenly reappeared, breathless and abashed. "Damn near forgot. This for you, Mr. Crane."

He rushed out and Larry read the flimsy. "Meet me Santa Fe soon as possible. Bad situation Southern New Mexico Territory. Will explain. Harriet sends regards and looks forward to Santa Fe. Jepson Reeves."

Larry folded the telegram. Why was it, he wondered, the mere mention of Harriet Reeves called her picture up so vividly in his mind?

He shrugged. He could just pack and catch the eastbound. He found his stride eagerly lengthening as he started toward the hotel.

Center Point Large Print
600 Brooks Road / PO Box 1
Thorndike ME 04986-0001 USA

(207) 568-3717

US & Canada:
1 800 929-9108
www.centerpointlargeprint.com